THE VIEW

FROM

THE TURNSPIT

SYLVIA DAVEY

ONE March 1567

Fifteen year old Will Randolph was pondering his position in the world and beginning to realise that having the time to be able to consider such matters in the first place was actually one of the good things about his job. He would never have chosen such work, but then, choice was not something he had been offered. Some people might consider it drudgery. He would probably have agreed, but although he was paid only a pittance, he at least wasn't whipped for slacking. He had seen that happen to some boys his age, and even to some adults.

It was true that there were lots of bad things. He had to sit long hours in this kitchen, full of steam and foul smelling burnt fat. There were two other kitchens down the corridor. One stank constantly of raw fish. They were pokey places in comparison to his, though he did like the smell of the freshly baked bread which drifted over every time he walked past the bakery. He had once thought he might prefer working there, until he realised that there was not much more than mixing and kneading going on. It was even more monotonous than what he did all day and at least there were people around him here who kept his brain awake. In any case, the bakery was just as hot as his own kitchen, with bread being turned out in continuous batches all day. Some of it was cheap and nasty stuff. That was the bread for the palace workers, whilst the royals and lords could feast on refined bannocks baked on griddles. The bread that was left at the end of the day was cut into thick slices and used as trenchers the next day. That bread had become solid by the next morning and you could sometimes break a tooth on it if you weren't careful. It was actually not really intended to be eaten, although some people were so hungry that they did. Its real use was as a platter, a trencher, for those people who couldn't afford their own platter or dish. It gathered up all the juices of the meat and vegetables and was actually not as bad as people made out. The soaked up mess from the meal gave its own particular flavour. Will knew that perfectly well as he had eaten his own trenchers and those abandoned by the less hungry many times. After all, he had been a growing lad. He still was.

Will's job was to keep turning the spit handle for the huge kitchen fire, keep it turning and turning all day, as the meats and poultry were cooking. Sometimes the boredom might well have broken his spirit if there hadn't been other people around. His ability to disguise a yawn was so well perfected now, that he rarely had his head biffed these days, though he was biffed for other sins on occasion. But he had also refined the art of avoiding the sudden, downward sweep of a hand in his direction. He generally could see it coming now. He didn't always know what the punishment was for, but since it hurt, he could now swerve out of the way with admirable skill.

Will had a seat, a little wooden stool under the great mantel stone of the fireplace. Standing and turning in this limited space were dangerous tasks. He had crashed into that mantel so many times and not only did it hurt but he came away each time with a head blackened by all the soot which lay in depth on the mantel itself and fell upon him in large quantities, no matter how much the mantel might have been scrubbed. There was also the red hot stinging of a hand on his cheek for clumsiness. A stinging hand was no fun when he was hot enough already. It was even worse when the hand was soiled with animal blood or grease and sometimes left chunks of the same in his hair. Not surprisingly he could smell his own aroma and that wasn't just because of his infrequent washing.

There was a huge great bale of wet hay in front of him which was supposed to keep him cool. He poured more cold water over it from time to time to maintain the dampness. He would pour water over his own head during hot summer days. He supposed that the hay did keep him cool, but there was no way of knowing in such heat. How could he know what it was like at the other end of the room where Jennet and Minnie were furiously chopping vegetables or where, across from him, Gillie was perfecting his sauces, caressing them with soft words of endearment which Will couldn't understand? He supposed the words were French because Gillie was French, but they were unlike any French sweet nothings Will had ever heard. Not that he had heard many, but he had on occasions unintentionally interrupted some amorous encounters behind curtains or in shadowy corners as he wandered the palace corridors. And yes, he had wandered palace corridors in France. He did remember some of his time there, though it was many years ago. Gillie... his name was really Gilbert ... had obviously been in France too, probably in some of the same places, though they had not known one another then. Gillie had learnt his profession in French kitchens and come over with Queen Mary when she had returned to the land of her birth after the death of her first husband, the King of France. That King, Francis 11, was a poor man ... well he was no more than a boy really and a sickly, weak one at that. Francis had died at the age of about sixteen, after only a few months as King. Will was pondering again. Poor Mary! Such a short time as Queen and then she had had to give up the civilised court of Paris for this backwater of Scotland. If Edinburgh was supposed to be the royal city of Scotland, then God help the rest of the country. Gillie must feel the loss too. His sauces were valued in France. They were not here, except by the Queen and her entourage. But Gillie loved his sauces beyond all else. His English, or rather his Scots, a language which sounded to Will like you were trying to clear your throat of some particularly thick muck, was hard to follow.

What Will did know, going back to his bale of hay, was that it gave off plumes of hot steam which rose into his face and up his nose and rendered his hair sodden and itchy. It didn't help that other kitchen staff would muss his hair up as they walked past. Perhaps they saw him scratching and wanted to help, but then everybody had lice of some sort around here and scratching was the least of his worries. He suspected that some of them were simply wiping their hands on him when the kitchen drying cloths were lost under a pan or lurking in the wood pile. His hair was long and thick and appropriate to the task. People also pushed his head forwards in their mussing so that he pitched into the very bale of hay which had caused the itching in the first place. He thus collected more scraps of hay to irritate him further. His face was permanently scratched and reddened; it never had time to heal. His face matched his hands, blistered in so many places and so often from the red hot iron of the spit. He'd been given some old rags to put over the handle but they kept falling off and sometimes even burnt over his fingers. And once or twice, they had leapt completely into flames themselves, caked as they were with grease. Bessie, one of the women in the kitchen gave him some comfrey salve now and again to rub on the sores at night. And if the fire didn't get him, the spitting fats from the roasting meats would spatter the rest of his body and ruin his clothes. Not that they could be called clothes as he covered himself in his oldest rags before setting foot in the hot, stifling hell he worked in.

So yes, he agreed that he did have time to think in the boredom of turning that spit handle all and every day. He even had a spit partner, Derry, the boy at the other end with his own similar instruments of torture. It could have been fun if they had been able to laugh together, mimic the other workers or enjoy whatever mischief the other palace workers got up to. But Derry was certainly not a conversationalist. He just kept turning that handle as if there was nothing else in the world. Will had tried to talk to him but there had never been anything forthcoming. He was no fun at all really. The lad was useful though. Without him, Will would never have had any free time. At least when it was quiet, Will could slope off and disappear for a while, whilst Derry kept everything turning. Will did the same for him.

But Will thought on and realised that perhaps having time to think had its dangers. A boy who had once sat in Will's place had been too immersed in his pondering and pitched himself forward too much, perhaps dozing or day-dreaming in another and better world. The hay had fallen into the fire. The boy had lost his balance and followed it into the burning mass. The mishap became a catastrophe. The poor wee fellow was, as the wags in the kitchen enjoyed telling, burnt to a cinder. He had certainly gone into another world, not necessarily the one he had been dreaming of. Not all the kitchen servants found the incident funny. That boy had been well known and liked by some of them. Will certainly didn't see the funny side of it, especially as it could have been him. But it was a hard world for all of them. After thinking too much, Will would become subdued. He would realise that his control was slipping and he would straighten his back for a while and set his mind back on his task. It was like waking up.

The other things Will realised he could do from his little alcove stool were listen and watch. He did a lot of those. They went with the thinking. Nearly every-one associated with Holyrood Palace came into the kitchens at some time. Even the Queen herself had come in once to thank them all for some service. The place may have been chokingly hot for those who worked there, but for those who could leave when they chose, it was a haven, cosy when snow lay on the ground, dry when you came in from a storm. And for the hungry, which meant most of the serv-ants, there was always something you could filch from under the nose of one of the cooks, even if it was only a tattered cabbage leaf from the waste pile. Will had to admit that he ate well, in spite of his meagre wage. He had seen the hovels that some of the citizens of Edinburgh called home and the so-called food that they lived off. He could at least al-ways cadge a morsel of bread to dip in the roasting drip tin or intercept a basket of waste before it went to the midden. There was usually a neepy top or some apple peelings in there somewhere that had missed going into the pottage or into a pie and he

14

also got a share of the leftovers from the high tables, some of that posh bread for example. He even crept back to his fire on really cold nights to sleep curled up alongside it and had been surprised to find so many of his fellow workers with the same idea.

The listening and watching were entertainments too. Those servants, who were able to roam freely about the building, could be guaranteed to return with whispering tales of goings on in remote chambers amongst the highers and betters. There were good mimics who kept them all laughing when they recognised some powdered and mincing lord, puffing himself up to gain attention. Some were able to talk about the town itself and retell the gossip they'd heard out there. There was always something going on and somebody who knew something, until in the end they all knew everything. Or thought they did. Even the almost high and mighty sometimes came in. They got cold and wet too, riding in from somewhere in the depths of the Scottish countryside. The kitchen staff all had the wisdom to keep their mouths shut where it mattered, when those high and mighty joined them. Tittle tattle was excellent merriment but it could also be perilous, especially at the moment when the royal world was in such a turmoil after the death of the Lord Darnley. Accusations could be wild and venomous and could endanger anyone stupid enough to interfere or repeat them. Will, like all the servants, valued his skin and kept out of the way, pressed safely into his little niche, as he listened to the outrageous language, the sweeping boasts, the outright lies. Listening was a diversion not to be missed, as long as you could keep your head down and feign to have heard nothing later. It was a skill most of the kitchen workers had acquired.

Like now, for instance. Just as Will was beginning to feel more bored than usual, the door opened and a huge man breezed in. Everyone knew him … it was Glennie, one of the woodcutters for the household fires, a bright and cheerful man, the size of an oak tree, with long knotted hair and oversized muscles.

His face was a mass of red bloated veins from work-ing in the drying wind and rain of the city's forests. Not only did Glennie and his men go out foraging for wood but they cut it too and brought it in to wherever it was required. It was needed in Will's kitchen every day for his own huge fire but also for the smaller ones that lined up in a row with counters over them at the other side of the enormous room. Pans bubbled constantly there with pottage or with Gillie inventing some fancy sauce. Glennie brought the wood and two young lads, younger than Will and Derry, trundled round the room keeping every fire fed. Will didn't know their names. They were called 'boy' as far as he could hear. They each answered to that whenever called. Glennie couldn't pass unno-ticed because of his bulk, but seeing him so often, people had grown to take his presence for granted. He managed to get everywhere except into the Queen's private rooms. She had her own servants for her fires, and her own kitchen too, for her visitors and personal staff. Today, it appeared that Glennie

17

had been into Edinburgh. He lived there somewhere with his wife and family tucked into a one bed-roomed apartment in a tenement. He had a voice as big as his body so that the whole kitchen missed nothing. He must have taken up most of the room in the pokey tenement wherever he lived.

'A bowl of pottage and some bread for me pains and I'll tell ye all of what's been going on in the town. A seat as well by the fire, if you please. It's fair drab and cold outside.'

Glennie's voice boomed whilst he waited. At length he made his announcement. 'There's been another placard.'

Everyone knew what he was referring to. They knew about the anonymous placards being set up on trees, on walls, all around the centre of Edinburgh. They had started in February, just a week after King Darnley's murder only a month or so ago. Their proclamations were wide ranging … that Lord Bothwell was Darnley's murderer; that the Queen had given her consent to the murder; that foreigners had been involved; that witchcraft had been worked on the Queen to make her wicked in her ways. Every one of the Queen's servants had had much to say, not to the Queen's face of course, but she must have known about the placards. Every corner rang with gossip. All had opinions but no-one had stepped forward to own the placards. And no one had stepped forward either in answer to the Queen's own proclamation that a reward of 2000 Scots pounds was offered to anyone who could identify Darnley's murderer. That was a lot of money. Everyone clamoured to tell whoever would listen who the murderer was but no one had any proof or the nerve to stand out from the massing crowds.

The hum of excitement rose as Glennie was begged to continue his tale, but the man relished his pottage and roared for more bread. He knew how to titillate an audience.

'Well, this is the best yet,' he said and received a chorus of frustration as people thought he was referring to the soup. They didn't care about the pottage.

19

The pottage simmered its way through every day of their lives. It was a thick soup made with anything available and it kept most of them alive, for want of something more substantial to eat. But they didn't value it.

'Ay, the best yet', and he paused again for effect.

'Away with ya,' shouted someone. 'If he's not going to tell us, take his food off of him.'

Glennie shielded his bowl and pulled an amicable and protective fist.

'The best placard yet,' he said finally. No –one was worried that his mouth was packed full of bread as he spoke. 'The Queen was naked as the day she was born. You know what I mean.' His sly and rascally grin raised a few eyebrows in his audience. 'Well-rounded dugs on her. That red brown hair curling round them to lure a man in. It's rough drawn, but the crown balanced on her head tells you it's her, right enough.'

Eyes widened and there were mutterings. Will knew that there were as many loved the Queen as there were to despise her. He remembered that it hadn't always been like this. She had been cheered into Scotland when she had first arrived back from France. She was still loved for her friendly and out-going personality but now hated by many for being a frivolous woman and a Catholic to boot. Even so, the placard was a disrespect which shamed them all. It was offensive and, though it was hard not to relish the story, it was not what a queen deserved. There was sniggering but mostly people were shocked.

Glennie waved them down with his breaded hand.

'Ah, there's more if you'll quieten yerselves.'

There was an instant resettling.

'Well, there she was as naked as she could be, save this … that her bottom half was a mermaid. A mermaid! Can you imagine? All tail she was, and with a hare to keep her company. The two of them looked to be frolicking together. You can guess my meaning.'

Another gasp as they all thought of the hare. Eve-ryone knew it for a fast breeding animal. The tale was that it did nothing all day but thrust forth time and time again, producing litter after litter. The insinuation was crude. Hares and rabbits were bred for food by every poor family with a bit of land so that they all knew the implications. But the hare was also the family crest of the Lord Bothwell's family. The placard was foully linking the Queen with Lord Bothwell and they all knew about him too. He was not a man to spare himself sexually when a woman was on offer. Even if the woman was not actually being offered. And the mermaid was an insult to Queen Mary herself. In spite of his youth, Will had heard the word often enough. He knew it was one of the many common words for a loose woman, a prostitute. The placard was a daring, but foul, insult.

Glennie swept out as fast as he had swept in, leaving the kitchen folk whispering and blethering amongst themselves, from the meanest of them to the ones supposedly in charge. They eventually had to be called back to their work. Will was too young for anyone to value his opinion but he knew what he thought and he knew he would learn more by listening than joining in. He sat there without speaking and, of course, Derry at the other end of the spit, never said a word. Will flattered himself that he probably had more knowledge of the wider world than any of the other servants in the kitchens. It was a good thing they didn't know his background or he would have been unduly pestered and teased. In the kitchen the turnspit was the lowest of the low, only a 'spit' above the 'boys'. He wasn't exactly scorned, but he wasn't cherished either. He was just Will Randolph and couldn't be expected to know anything. But, he thought with smug satisfaction, there was more to Will Randolph than they realised.

TWO

Will Randolph took his name from the Lord Thomas Randolph, who was Queen Elizabeth's emissary in Scotland, the man who wrote to Lord Cecil, Elizabeth's Secretary of State, to keep her English Majesty informed of all that was going on in the Scottish kingdom. Everyone knew him for an important man, a man at the centre of most of what was going on at the court and beyond. Will wasn't Lord Randolph's son; at least he didn't think he was. He didn't know for sure. He didn't know who his father was, but he did know that his mother had worked for his Lordship for many years and had 'borrowed' Lord Randolph's name when he'd been born, for want of a genuine name for the father. She obviously knew who the father was, but it was a secret that she chose to keep to her heart. William was perfectly aware that he was her bastard son and it usually didn't bother him too much.

Maddy, Will's mother, had been born in Reculver on the Kent coast, a village with not much to recommend it except its fishing and the fact that the Romans had once had a fort there. There were a few bits of Roman wall to see, but little else. The Romans didn't mean much to most of the villagers. If the word meant anything, it was probably the city in Italy that they brought to mind. They had very little sense of history that went beyond their grandmothers and grandfathers and possibly a few generations beyond that. There was no school in the village and no books or pictures. Their concern was how to get through each day with enough to eat and no sickness. The Roman galleys, which had once sailed their own fishing seas, were less real to them than the sea monsters local tales talked about.

Maddy's family had been 'respectable', the meaning of which was understood among most of the local families as doing honestly what your neighbours did so that you didn't draw unworthy attention. They were moderately less poverty stricken than their neighbours, but the bright girl Maddy was able enough to realise that she could only look forward to more of the same as she grew up and there was always a yearning within her for something different. That yearning increased as she grew older. Heavy rains and winter storms lashed at the exposed village every year and the houses and fishermen's huts at its outer edges took the brunt of the tempests. Over the years some of them began slowly eroding into the sea. Maddy watched as houses slipped down the cliffs. It was a fascination for those whose houses weren't doing the slipping and when the last stones disappeared onto the rocks and shingle below, it was even a strange satisfaction for some, especially for those who had had the foresight, more likely luck, to build further inland. Parts of the church, the graveyard headstones sank into the waves alongside them. Each year there were fewer headstones left to see.

The repeated drama these scenes caused amongst the population gave Maddy the excuse she needed. It had taken her some time to persuade her family that she should go, but in the end she had taken herself off and found work in service a few miles away in a small place called Badlesmeer, which happened to be the family home of Lord Randolph's lineage. She had simply gone from door to door knocking around the back of any large farmhouses or mansions on her way to wherever, and asked at each one for work. Badlesmeer was the one which took her on. She'd looked neat and clean and had henceforth kept herself so. She'd started out as a general skivvy but because of that cleanliness and her fastidious attention to her work, she had risen through the ranks until she became a general maid and keeper and repairer of the family's clothes. She eventually managed some of the younger workers, those who washed and tidied away the clothes, tossed carelessly aside for someone else to pick up. She had regularly been on hand to sew young Thomas Randolph's stockings together whenever he'd put his knees through. You would not have guessed that the dour man he was now had ever been that young boy, the lad who climbed trees to raid birds' nests, and jumped brooks that were just a bit too wide.

Young Thomas was not much older than Madeleine herself, as she now wanted to be known, and Will had originally thought that he was the result of some dalliance between his mother and Lord Randolph. As he grew older and daring enough to ask about such things, his mother had laughed and told him that Lord Thomas was an honourable man who had never laid such a finger on her. But Lord Thomas had gone off to study in Oxford and Paris and had met a lot of people who had no such qualms, and it was one of those friends, visiting at Badlesmeer, who had conquered Madeleine's naivety with promises and assurances, and been her undoing. This was the tale she told and she would give nothing more away. Will rather liked the idea of imagining himself the son of a romantic and gallant Frenchman from Paris. He rejected the possible lying Frenchman of his mother's tale. The lying or gallant lover was long gone before Madeleine's predicament was discovered and Thomas, now a Protestant of somewhat naïve and prudish disposition, was mortified to learn that it was his friend who had led the innocent Madeleine into the sins of the flesh. He had known that the fellow was an established philanderer and had never thought to warn her away from him or keep his debauched friend away from her. He felt that the unhappy predicament was all his fault so that when his family wanted Madeleine turned out of the household, as was the custom in those days for wayward unmarried mothers, he argued to save her and took her on as his own particular servant. She had been with him ever since.

Lord Randolph had kept a sharp eye on Madeleine henceforth with his future visiting friends, wary of over-friendly ladies' men with flattering words and illicit intentions. Will's mother had told him that Lord Randolph was as far from a Lothario as he could be. He seemed not to know the meaning of the word romance and in any case, his mother had learnt her lesson. The over-serious Lord became totally dependent on Madeleine and she knew that was a far more precious sort of love.

Will was not entirely convinced by this tale and from time to time looked slyly at Lord Randolph and continued to wonder. But he did think that if Lord Randolph had been his parent, he would surely have wanted his son to learn to read and write. The fact that such arrangements had never been made for Will to learn was fairly convincing evidence for him that he wasn't a neglected son, but a well-treated servant's brat. This still bubbled up as a resentment in him from time to time, though not often, as he felt it led him nowhere. Yes, he felt his disadvantage in the world, but he had trained himself to rise above it. He may not have learnt to read and write but he had trained himself to have an excellent memory.

There wasn't much to remember in the Edinburgh kitchen where he currently found himself, but the murder of Lord Darnley and that fellow Rizzio before him had stirred things up everywhere in the palace and the town. There was a lot to think about and he enjoyed the thinking. It was like a puzzle to sort out and it kept the boredom away.

The Kent neighbourhood had considered Thomas Randolph a fool for being so soft towards the girl Madeleine, but as time went on, he showed he was anything but a fool. He prospered, became a notary, then principal of one of the Oxford Colleges until he had to resign or face prosecution for his Protestant religion under Queen Mary Tudor, old King Henry's eldest daughter. Queen Mary, a strong Catholic herself, was trying to force Catholicism back onto her subjects and getting rid of those equally strong minded people who refused to cooperate. The world had become even more cruel than usual. There were burnings. Randolph was one of those strong minded people who refused to co-operate and took himself into exile in France to avoid his own persecution. Quite unexpectedly, he found himself being appointed as Queen Elizabeth's representative in Germany when, as Mary's sister and daughter of the old King, she came to the throne on Mary's death. The rules about religion changed again. Who could keep up with them?

But all the time, even abroad, eventually in Paris, Randolph had taken Madeleine with him everywhere, passing her off as his housekeeper, a widow with a baby, then child, and then boy. William was kept out of the way as much as possible. Maybe that's all his mother was, a housekeeper, thought Will again, but wherever he lived, he knew there were whisperings and he recognised undertones of gossip which Lord Randolph, in some airy cloud, seemed totally unaware of. Lord Randolph was a serious man who rarely laughed and, Will thought, took himself far too seriously. Yet, he had provided Will with a home and seemed to care in some strange way for his mother.

Will had been brought to Scotland when Lord Randolph had journeyed north from London to negotiate around the Queen of Scots' marriage. Lord Randolph's remit had been to ensure that Queen Mary of Scots married the right person as far as the interests of the English throne were concerned. Will had tried to understand who the 'right person' might be. Queen Elizabeth of England apparently didn't want the future King of Scotland, whoever he might turn out to be, to be any kind of threat to her own power. Will's mother must somehow have taught her son all about the importance of watching and listening and, working for Lord Randolph, she had been at the centre of so much of what was worth watching and listening to. Lord Randolph met with so many important people and Will often wondered if his mother was above listening at doors. She always seemed to be as well informed about things as Lord Randolph himself, in spite of the fact that she always argued that Lord Randolph never told her anything. Will, consequently, was as informed as the pair of them. He had loved sitting with his mother, listening whilst she gossiped with other members of Lord Randolph's household. He remembered everything he had heard.

Queen Mary Stewart had eventually married the Lord Darnley, the perfect choice it had at first appeared, a handsome, elegant and wealthy English man. He had come up from England and presented himself as first in line for Queen Mary's hand and next in line for the English crown. Will didn't rightly know how the young man could be a royal heir in both England and France; something about his mother being some descendant of Henry V111. He had met the man's father, the Earl of Lennox, who had come into the kitchen one morning having missed a meal in the great hall. He was another Stewart and had married another descendant of the same Henry. So that made Mary and Lord Darnley something like cousins. He wasn't sure of the exact relationship.

Darnley had been an utter charmer and nobody had seen beyond that at first. Will could understand how the Queen had been flattered in both her position and her ambition. She had always seemed to believe she was the rightful claimant to the English throne. In fact, when she had married her French husband, Henry 11, the French king at the time, had proclaimed them both King and Queen of England too.

Lord Randolph had said privately that she was asking for trouble if she repeated that too often. In fact, some people would later say that she was more interested in being the future Queen of England than in being the present Queen of Scotland. The fact that Darnley was a Catholic suited Queen Mary too, though the Protestant Queen Elizabeth might not have been so pleased.

The marriage had gone sour almost from the beginning and Will also knew all about that from his mother. Lord Randolph had no good words for the man after the first euphoria. He almost spat when he talked about him. As for Lord Randolph himself, he was still unmarried and Will also wondered what that signified since the man was getting on in years now. He must have been at least forty. Which seemed very elderly to Will. He was thinking of his mother again. Didn't Lord Randolph need an heir? His mother must surely be more than just a loyal servant?

THREE

A voice broke Will's remembrances.

'What do you think of that then?'

It was Jennet holding out a drink of water. He saw she had offered one to Derry before him.

'What?'

'Glennie's news about the placard.'

Will shrugged. 'The placards? Well they're all much the same, aren't they? They don't stay up long, but I suppose they're seen by enough people before they get taken down so that the damage is done. The Queen could do with setting someone on watch to catch whoever it is. She has enough serv-ants. She could use her officers of the guard. Is it one person or a few? She doesn't seem to be doing anything about them. They are destroying her reputation. Will thought privately that the Queen was a bit slow. If he'd had anything to do with it, the offender would have been caught already.

'Do you think it's true what they say about her?'

Jennet's voice was low, almost whispering, but

Will shook his head. Hearing someone else talking about putting up placards secretly at night was one thing but making judgements in a kitchen full of people was another. He trusted Jennet. She had been working in the kitchen almost as long as he had. And she was a bonny lass. He laughed at himself. He was talking like a Scotsman now. Bonny? Dark long hair, which she tied up with string when she was in the kitchen. And dark eyes too. She could almost have passed for French. She was the general skivvy his mother had once been and as such he felt a fondness for her. And she was the same age as he was too. He liked everyone who worked in the kitchen, but he was sensible enough to realise that he should always be on his guard. There were lot of ears ready to entrap someone for the reward of a meagre coin. He didn't trust that Derry, whose eyes shifted every time Will looked his way. Will's eyes now told Jennet that he was being wary and so she said simply that she would see him later. It was not a tryst. He generally helped her carry the waste baskets to the midden at the end of the day. That's when they could talk. There were two girls who chopped vegetables all day for the pottage. The other girl, Minnie, was well built with thickened arms and Will felt she was quite capable of carrying her own vegetable waste to the midden. Actually, Jennet was equally capable, but Will was happy to fool himself. He liked Jennet's dark-hair and he didn't want to see her struggle. It didn't occur to him that there was very little waste for either girl to carry since every smallest morsel of the vegetables was used for the pottage. Even rotten chunks were cooked for long enough so that their origins were indistinguishable in the pottage mass. There were always two pots of the stuff simmering away, yesterday's and todays. Yesterday's remains became the beginnings of today's when the kitchen started up every morning. It was set to reheat before anything else was done. It was a wonder there were not more people complaining of gut rot. It must have been something to do with the boiling or the long hours simmering. The pottage seemed to look the same all year, whatever vegetables went into it. You could never tell the difference. Old bits of bread, left over bits of meat, were all thrown in as well to thicken the liquid and stretch it further.

Later, the midden stench hung in the air around Jennet and Will, but sitting at some distance from it, the fumes were bearable and your nose got used to them. There was an old log to accommodate them nearby. It had been polished by the bottom of every person who had sat on it. It was often a place for the sharing of dreams and secrets for those who had smoothed it, but for Will and Jennet it was no more than a place to gossip and giggle. People came and went to the midden but in the growing darkness it was easy to ignore the two low-borns who didn't count for much to those who could make them out. They kept their voices soft all the same.

Jennet didn't wait to repeat her question.

'Do you think it's true about the Queen? That she *has* been consorting with Bothwell? And so soon after the Lord Darnley's death?'

Will nodded. Or, he thought, that Bothwell had been certainly chasing her. Which wasn't quite the same thing.

'But how could she?' Jennet puzzled. 'The Queen was guarded after the killing of Rizzio. They had been trying to kill her. That's what she said. And Rizzio took the blows in her place. I wouldn't want anyone near me.'

Will knew about Rizzio. The man had been selected to be a musician in the Queen's private music group. He played the lute and had a supposedly wonderful singing voice. Will had never heard him play or sing, but he did know that the fellow was Italian and had become very influential in the court, causing much rivalry and jealousy. He'd also heard him called a sly foreigner and that he was even suspected of being a papal spy. Randolph certainly hadn't liked him.

'No,' said Will now. 'The killing was for Rizzio, no doubt about it. It was planned by many.'

Will was quite firm, as Randolph had also been. Will couldn't remember the names of those lords who had been involved in the plotting, but he knew that Lord Darnley, Queen Mary's own husband, had been one of them. Queen Bess in England seemed to know about the plan before the murder ever took place. Everybody had seemingly known about it. Everybody except Rizzio, the Queen and a few of her followers. Queen Mary had always been safe. Will knew that for sure. The jealousy was her husband's; Darnley and those lords who assisted him thought to gain power thereby. Even Darnley himself was really for naught in the planning. He was being manipulated himself. Will had heard Lord Randolph argue as much and he thought it was right. Lord Randolph had said that Rizzio had accepted bribes when people wanted an audience with the Queen for whatever reason. He had over-reached himself. He was a greedy gatekeeper.

'I didn't like Rizzio,' Jennet continued. 'He seemed a slimy, fawning creature to me, but he could have been dismissed, couldn't he? Why did they have to murder him?'

'The Queen would never have allowed dismissal. He was her appointment after all. What right had they to tell her who she should choose as her servants? That was her opinion. She *is* their monarch after all. And you're right. The man was a weasel. He fawned on her too much. She swam in his flattery. He was an Italian. Do you know what they're like?' Will had as many prejudices as the next man but scarcely realised it.

He didn't wait for an answer. 'The Italians know how to woo a woman. Or they think they do. They're like the French. It was what she was used to from her time at the French courts. From when she was Queen of France. She had grown to expect it there, but she never got such flattery here in Scotland. Never from her husband, at any rate, after the first few weeks. The people here are a rough lot. What do they know about romance and flattery?' Will spoke as if he knew all about such things. He went on. 'Rizzio was too valuable to her. It wasn't just their singing and making music together that she cared about. He was the one person she felt was her own to confide in.'

'But she is guarded now. How can Bothwell reach her at night? How can what the placards say be true?'

'Does it have to be at night? But let me tell you a tale. Did you ever hear about what happened to Chastelard?'

Jennet was shaking her head.

'Well, he was one of the servants the Queen brought back from France with her when she returned to Scotland. Like Gillie, you know, who makes the sauces. I think he was a page. Well, this Chastelard managed to get into Mary's chamber at night, even with her guards on duty. Perhaps he was invited at first? Who knows? She behaved with him as she did with Rizzio. She was seen treating him as too much the familiar, with kisses on his neck and a warmth that was not worthy of him. I'm not saying it went further than that but … but he was just a valet or a Page, nothing more..

It seems the man believed the Queen was in love with him. He hid under her bed one night and was found by the grooms and banished. But the silly fool was too enamoured by now to desist. So then, he followed when she went on progress to Fife and entered her room again. He said later he was just trying to beg forgiveness for the first incident, but the Queen seemed to believe he was returned to rape her. Her step brother Lord Moray was nearby and, hearing her cries, took hold of the fellow. Mary shouted that he should thrust his dagger into the villain.'

Jennet gasped. Will had always thought the girl was a little in awe of Queen Mary, her laughing charm, her beauty, the very majesty of her. He could understand that. Jennet was like so many of the poorer people, ready to kneel before wealth and privilege. Will flattered himself that he had the wisdom to see through all that. But he was amongst the lowly himself and really had done no more than listen to what his mother had learnt from overheard conversations. He had taken on his mother's words and called them his wisdom. It was a wisdom that was largely borrowed and he didn't like to acknowledge that.

'And what did my Lord Moray do?' Jennet was both horrified and exited by the story. Her eyes were glowing. And Will was flattered by her attention. It was a pleasure to flaunt his so called superior knowledge. 'Did he kill the valet? I haven't heard this story before, probably because it didn't happen in Edinburgh.'

Will enjoyed the moment. He kept her waiting for the answer, as if he were searching his memory, trying to remember the story he knew. 'No, but Chastelard was later beheaded in the market place in St Andrews. Do you not remember that? Mary refused all his pleas for mercy.'

Jennet gasped again. Perhaps she had thought the story was going to have a happy ending, another tale of love and romance concerning the favoured Queen of Scots. A tale to please the ladies. But Will was quick to enlighten her.

'So you see, the Queen is not the gentle and gracious lady people make her out to be,' he said. 'She cried out for that valet to be stuck like a pig. She learnt to be hard and cruel in France under her uncles, the Ducs de Guise.'

'Her mother's brothers?'

'Ay, the brothers of Mary of Guise, our Mary's mother, our last Queen and then our Queen Regent when Mary's father died just after she had been born. Mary has been a Queen since she was a week old. Her expectations cannot help but be royal. Nor can she be other than Catholic. Her French relatives, the Guises, are all fanatical Catholics.'

Lord Randolph had hated the Guise brothers, the Duc de Guise and the Cardinal of Lorraine. He had condemned them for nearly everything which had gone wrong in France. He said they were cruel and ruthless and that if that was being Catholic he wanted none of it.

'I have another story for you,' Will said, unwilling to turn away from Jennet's glowing admiration. 'Those same Guise uncles, hanged Protestants from the wall of the Chateau d'Amboise. There was a lot of fighting between the Protestant and the Catholics when Mary was growing up in France. In those days, the royal family ate in the dining room in the Chateau, right next to where the bodies of the hanged men were rotting outside. Mary was with her royal husband, the French one, the Dauphin. She must have known about all of that, all about what had gone on. God, she must have been able to smell the bodies. She must have seen them hanging there. Can you imagine eating your dinner alongside all those swinging corpses? The flies, the stench? So, it's no wonder that Mary can be vicious in how she behaves. She's seen it all. It doesn't seem to touch her.'

Jennet was breathing hard, her head full of the story, if not full of the stench as well. Will enjoyed her distaste and went on. 'And Mary saw how the French behaved at court too. So much luxury. So much bad behaviour, the women as well as the men. I heard all about it when my mother worked in Paris. I wasn't supposed, to but I did. I listened to all the gossip. Much more lewd behaviour than here. And it's bad enough here, don't you think? And Mary seems to prefer those foreigners to her Scottish nobles. She draws them to her and shuns the Scottish lairds. So you can't blame the lairds for being annoyed. It's their country here. She doesn't seem to learn either. Rizzio was unpopular because he was a foreigner. So, what's the first thing she does after he's killed? She appoints his brother in the man's place. Foolish or what? And you wonder how that Bothwell could reach her if he wanted to. We are innocents, you and I. There's a hidden world around us. '

'But surely she has the right to appoint her own people? After all, she is the Queen. And if the Queen wants Bothwell, surely she can have him visit? Do you think she does want him?'

Will shrugged. How did he know what the Queen wanted? He wasn't that clever. Jennet was still considering. '

'But I did feel sorry for her with Darnley. He was a foul creature. Why did she marry him?'

'You saw him. What did you think of him?'

'That he was as foul as I just said. But I thought he was lovely at first, gracious, handsome, equal in nobility to her. Such lovely clothes. I could understand how she was taken by him. He was tall too. She needed someone tall, her being so high herself.'

'But that was part of the trouble. He thought himself high in everything. He thought he was her equal when he wasn't really. Yes, he had high born ancestors but Mary was actually the daughter of a King, and a Queen herself. He fed off the flatterers who surrounded him. He thought he should be made full King when he married our Majesty. And when she didn't give him that position, his pride became intolerable. He was like a child in a sulk, stamping his foot. He insulted people, threatened them for naught. He was probably seeing himself as heir to the throne of England one day. All the other heirs had gone and if Elizabeth was barren, Mary was next in line. As Mary's husband, he would rule England.'

Jennet had her own piece to add. 'I know that he drank too much. I saw him drunk myself a few times in the corridors. He once stretched out to grab my dugs as I passed, but I ducked out of his reach. Was it true that as well as chasing other women he went after the bodies of other men?'

Will frowned. Again, he was largely repeating what he'd heard from his mother via Lord Randolph. Lord Randolph probably had some protection for what he said as a representative from another country. Will didn't, and he wondered whether he was going too far now. It might be dangerous accusing the man of something most people considered an abomination. They certainly thought it was in Presbyterian Scotland. But the man Darnley was dead and it was Jennet who had spoken first. The rumours were rife in Edinburgh anyway. He was cautious. It was just gossip and rumour to him but Randolph had hated the man so much that he had believed it himself.

'I don't know for sure. It would seem so. He didn't catch syphilis from the Queen at any rate.'

That surprised Jennet. She had obviously not known that Darnley had suffered from syphilis. In fact, she was not even sure what syphilis was. She had the impression that it was some new ailment that had travelled to England from far off lands across the sea. Everyone said that it was to do with sex and that you caught it by having sex with someone who already had it. She thought it was to do with sleeping with lots of different people. The Church said it was God's punishment. But Will was still talking. He didn't notice the girl's shocked face.

'He was not worthy of the Queen anyway, but she doted on him. That's why the placards talk of witchcraft. The Queen was thought to have been bewitched in some way. Why else would she love him? People said that during his last illness he had to wear some sort of veil over his face to hide the pitted pock marks eating into his skin. And his breath was foul. That's what syphilis does to you. He was ugly and stank. He kept having to have baths to rid him of the smell. How could our Queen love that? '

'It seems that I am an innocent in the world,' said Jennet, her face screwing up tightly in disgust. 'I know nothing of such things. People said that his illness was just the measles. Are you sure that you are not just telling a tale?'

'I don't think so. It's what I heard. How could the Queen love him when he looked and behaved like that? I think she must have been pretending.'

Will could not admit the source of his information. Sometimes he wondered if Randolph, in his dislike of Darnley and the ways of the court, and indeed in his disapproval of Queen Mary herself, was not too harsh in his judgements. Perhaps Lord Randolph had painted a blacker picture than was true? And perhaps he was at fault now for being too ready to believe him? And, he thought, too ready to repeat what he had been told. He was forgetting himself in his showing off.

The sky had darkened fully now and Will felt he ought to be bringing this conversation to an end. He felt some embarrassment in talking about such things with a girl and in any case, the cold was creeping into his body. He was still in his turnspit rags and he didn't want other people to see him and be able to work out that he was merely one of the palace's inferior servants.

Being brought up in Lord Randolph's household had given Will a pride that should not really have been his. Up to his working in the kitchen, his life had been relatively easy so that the rags were felt as a source of shame and he wanted to get out of them. They brought him no warmth either. February had been chilling and there had been no improvement now that they were in March. He didn't want to sit there any longer. He saw the disappointment on

Jennet's face. He felt as if his superiority in knowing so much more than her about the great building behind them and the lives going on within was somehow a credit to him. He knew really that it was not. She was always so interested in what he had to say and he knew he was taking advantage of her innocence. She had a father working in Edinburgh somewhere but Will had never met him and she almost never talked about him. She seemed to be a little lost soul in the world. In a way, he felt sorry for her.

'Come on,' he said now. 'Let's return these baskets to the kitchen and see what's left to eat in the great hall. After all, we've been making it all day. We ought to be able to enjoy some of it. Let's hope they've kept a good fire going too. My bones are ice after being out here.'

The great hall was where people like Will and Jennet ate and slept. Most servants had pallets which they could spread out at night, although many slept on the floor rushes, rolled up in a cloak if they had one. The lords and sometimes their ladies slept and ate there too and even the Queen herself came to eat in the hall on special days, for a banquet or some such, but her food was much more various and more carefully prepared and presented. The servants rarely got to so much as sniff at the meat, poultry and puddings which were carried up to the top table in full view of the crowded underlings. At least Will and Jennet sometimes got to taste the leftovers, even if they were coldly congealed. Most of those people with eyes drooling over the dishes they saw passing up to their betters went to bed more hungry for knowing what they missed. The unaccustomed richness would probably have made them ill anyway.

Jennet was called over to sit with some friends but Will didn't want to join them. Normally he would have searched out his mother, though he rarely sat with her. She now mixed in a world above his but they always acknowledged each other and would sometimes meet on Sundays or other special days. She would bring him new clothes... well, they were new to him, but he couldn't wear some of the noble hand me downs she brought as they would have looked so out of place next to the turnspit fire. Questions would have unsettled him. He chose what he fancied and his mother adapted them for him. Small sums of money were passed on too, but he mostly squirreled those away, for who knew how his fortunes might turn? He had scraped out a small space into the brickwork alongside where he sat by the fire. He had blackened it over with soot to make it look as old as the brickwork itself. It was a pokey place but then, his hoard was only that of a pauper. It was as safe as he could make it. Who knew when he might need it? The way he spoke made him so obviously English and being English was not necessarily advantageous in the twisting and turning prejudices of the Scottish court. After all, Darnley had been English and everyone had hated him. Even the Queen in the end, even though she had married him. It hadn't taken her long to dig down to his real character. It seemed to be a general rule that the Scots disliked the English and the English disliked the Scots. Will didn't tell or even want people to know who his mother worked for. They thought he was knowledgeable because of his own wit and intelligence and Will enjoyed that they thought that. Sometimes, he wondered if he actually was more intelligent than some of the halfwits he came across in the palace. He didn't rate many of them. They were like cattle and accepted everything they were told until they lost patience sometimes and set about one another. They were such an argumentative lot. There was so much plotting and scheming amongst the lords that the tensions seemed to spill out amongst them all.

William's hope was that one day he would find a way out of the place. He remembered England. At least he thought he did. So much cleaner and more civilised than this pisspot Scotland where everybody seemed to be fighting everyone else. The lords and lairds set no example. They seemed to be just a set of thugs looking to impose their own rules. He knew

Lord Randolph thought the same. And there were Lord Randolph's ideas again, so well absorbed that Will now felt they were his own.

Will knew his mother wouldn't be there tonight. He missed seeing her though, even if only for a smile in passing. She had always kept herself at a distance from him for his protection and they had always met discreetly. Lord Randolph was not entirely trusted at the court and had finally been discovered passing on money to some of the Queen's Lairds who were plotting to rise up against her. Will didn't really know much about all that, though he did know that the Lord Moray, the Queen's step brother, was one of the rebel ringleaders, the others merely names heard in whispered comments around the palace … Rothes, Kirkcaldy, Chatelherault, Argyll, Glencairn. And all supported by their clansmen. He was right to fear them. They respected no rules. They objected to Mary's Catholicism, thinking she was going to impose the mass on them, though Will had learned, again via Lord Randolph, that it was more likely that Moray, in particular, was more interested in his position at court than in his religion. Moray had been the leader of Scotland as James V's oldest bastard son until Mary had returned from France and displaced him. Mary was the only legitimate heir, though her father had had several bastard sons and daughters. Moray's resentment must have blossomed at such a come-down. The Queen had scarcely noticed, fully trusting her half-brother when it was patently obvious to everyone but her that his only care was for himself. Will didn't take to Moray, even though the man was supposed to be in the faction which supported Queen Bess, the English faction. He was a dark, fearsome and secretive looking man who seemed to have his own designs on the Queen and yet he was never anywhere he shouldn't be when suspicions were being rumoured. He scowled too much for Will.

And then there was John Knox. People had listened to him far too much. Will was a Protestant himself but even he couldn't stomach the bigoted preaching which poured forth from John Knox's, loud-mouthed threats of hell and damnation for anyone who stepped out of his line of thinking. The man was the founder of the Presbyterian Church of Scotland, the Kirk of Edinburgh and everyone seemed to go in fear of him. Will had heard him preach. Everyone was allowed time on Sundays to go to the Kirk. Will supposed that Catholics could go to mass instead but there weren't many of those, except perhaps Kitty and Gillie. From the preaching, Will had observed that Knox seemed to hate women or at least argued that they should know their place. He proclaimed that Mary, as a woman monarch, was a violation of the divine order of things. Worse, she was a Catholic and, therefore, an abomination. Another abomination! Will smiled at the thought that this man, who must be at least fifty and ugly more than handsome, had now gone and married a young sixteen year old girl as his second wife. He'd be having fun in bed even if he did think women were monstrous creations of temptation and to be avoided.

The old goat! Knox's first wife had been a young maid too. Had he worn her out? People laughed and nudged one another and Will understood why.

Randolph hadn't been handing over his own money to support the rebels. It had come from Queen Bess in London ... £3000, he'd heard. That was an awful lot of money and when Will thought more deeply, he supposed it was definitely a form of treason. Randolph had provided money to help an uprising against a lawful monarch. Mary had been furious and rightly so, thought Will, however much he was supposed to be on Randolph's side. Mary had ridden out with her own men to challenge the rebels and they had been dispersed. The rebels hadn't had as much support as they had anticipated and the English money didn't stretch as far as it had needed to.

Randolph had been called in to stand before Mary and been severely reprimanded and then banished. Another smile from Will. Randolph hadn't gone far, only to Berwick on the border with England, where he seemed to be as informed as usual about what was going on at the Scottish court. Will had heard his name whispered amongst the gossip and tittle-tattle that surrounded him. There were probably more members of the court in Berwick and therea-bouts than in Holyrood now, all of them with their informants and couriers riding to and fro as they schemed about their next move. And Will's mother was with them, or at least with Lord Randolph.

Will wondered if Randolph would ever be allowed back into Scotland. Will hadn't been able to go with his mother and with Lord Randolph this time. His mother had found him this job in the kitchen. Was it really the best she could do for him? He suspected that, as he was now older, Lord Randolph was prob-ably thinking that Will ought to be making his own way in life and consequently pushing his mother in certain directions. She may have had no choice. Per-haps Will was becoming more expensive or possibly even a nuisance? Always there, always under the Lord's feet? Perhaps that was how the Lord felt? In his more miserable moments, Will felt like he had been ditched, brought up to expect more from life and now as desperate as any other poor person in Edinburgh.

Will couldn't see a way out. Berwick might only have been a few miles away but it could have been a hundred, since Will had no way of getting there. He had no address for his mother and in any case, he couldn't write. She couldn't write either. She might even have moved on to elsewhere by now. She could be back in London for all he knew. Lord Randolph never seemed to stay in one place for very long. That was the impression Will had from his younger days.

So, without his mother, Will felt bereft. It was the first time he had been so alone in the world. He found it hard to believe that she had just gone. And without Lord Randolph, Will would have little news to impress Jennet from now on. He would miss that. He had been beginning to get interested in all the wiles and schemes of those above him. There were no such intrigues in the kitchen. Nobody had the time. They were always working and it was too hot.

FOUR

Some weeks later, Will was in the kitchen coaxing the fire back into life. Everyone had to be back into work by four in the morning. It wasn't always light and sometimes in the winter, it was as dark as the night. Everyone still carried their sleep on them and moved so deliberately, as if they had to think about where they stepped. Well, actually they did! The corridors were supposed to be swept and cleaned each night but it was sometimes a cursory job and in the semi-darkness, so many things were missed. It wasn't just the smell of urine which could be distressing. There were other unpleasant things you could step in. People sometimes relieved themselves wherever they could find a quiet place. Vomit was the worst.

The kitchen fires had been kept dozing through the night by one of the 'boys' and now they just had to be fed again to get them back to cooking heat. Will went with the John Parlick the chief cook to the Flesh Room to collect the meats which were to be cooked that day. They passed the Wet Room where all the fish were hung or kept in tubs of salt. Fresh fish were brought in from tanks in the royal grounds. Will helped cut the sides of meat to size and then he had to set about trussing them onto the roasting spikes… chickens, ducks, plovers, swans and the like. The metal rods of the spit had been cleaned the night before when the grease was still soft and any burnt matter came away easily.

Will had just begun trussing the chickens when a page came through with a message. There would be no main meal for the court at ten o clock today. Pottage and other simple foods, bread, some cheese, would be available for the servants but the court would eat properly again later than the usual four o' clock. Possibly after six o'clock. The kitchen had to have food ready for then. Will was told to finish trussing the meats and then leave them covered away from the fire to put on to cook when he returned. That, he was told, would be around three o'clock. 'When he returned' meant that he was being given some free time. Jennet had looked up hopefully when she had heard that but she was disappointed. Her job of chopping up the left overs and any old meats or vegetables which couldn't be served separately was relentless. They all went into the pottage which was always available. She got even less free time than Will.

Will wasn't sorry. He mostly liked his own company and didn't want to be hampered by anyone else, especially a girl. Girls were a hindrance. You had to look after them, give them your full attention. They expected it. Jennet was pretty and good company sometimes but the prettiness would attract attention. He liked her but he didn't want to be bothered with that. Defending her honour against the eager lads of the town could lead you into scrapes or worse. He knew he was a skinny thing in comparison to some of the big muscled lads of Edinburgh. He'd met some of those. So, he was glad to skip off on his own, though he did wonder why there was to be no main meal that day.

He found out soon enough even before he went into Edinburgh. The Queen, he was told, was ill again. It seemed to him that she was always feeling ill or faint these days. Will felt that she needed to toughen up. He wasn't very sympathetic. She'd had her baby. What else had she to be ill about? Being ill all the time meant people were taking advantage of her weakened state. The gossips had been out and about as usual, telling everyone that without David Rizzio, or the Lord Darnley or her brother the Earl of Moray, the Queen was lost. She needed a man to make decisions for her. That was probably why she hadn't done anything to pursue justice for the death of Darnley, the King. She didn't even have her baby with her to take her mind off things, the child, son of Mary and Lord Darnley, who had been born shortly after the murder of Rizzio. That might have taken her out of herself and given her despair something to think of beyond herself. But the child had been sent to the royal nursery at Stirling. Into the open space, had stepped the Lord Bothwell, hollowing out a comfortable niche for himself. The man had always been around and he did seem to be a more loyal follower than most of the men at court. But the Queen was turning towards him more and more, often without seeming to realize that this was the man whom her people felt was the chief suspect for the murder of her husband. After all, he was the man named in all those placards in Edinburgh. Will heard questions being asked. Did the Queen not care? Did she even know what people were saying about him? Bothwell was becoming powerful. Step warily, Will told himself. Say nothing.

But the real reason for the late evening meal, as he was later able to work out, was that Bothwell was to be tried that day and all the courtiers who could, would be attending the trial. It promised to be an exciting entertainment. The Queen's illness meant that she would not be attending. Will suspected that her illness might have been feigned to avoid having to be present. Will had heard nothing about this trial. Already he was missing Lord Randolph. He would

have known the date, the time, the names of the witnesses, everything, if Randolph had been around.
His mother would have been listening and passing
on the information. He did, however, know that
Darnley's father, Lord Lennox, had been loud in his
demands for vengeance since the murder of his son.
He had cried his complaints, proclaimed his son's
murder everywhere. Everyone in Edinburgh must
have heard him. It had seemed at first that nothing
was being done, that the Lord Lennox was being ignored. But then, someone had pointed out that the
queen was in mourning and that, by tradition, that
would have to last forty days. Nothing could be done
until the period of mourning was at an end, though
the King had already been buried in the vaults of the
chapel royal. Bodies couldn't be left unattended for
so long. It was unhealthy.

Will remembered the funeral. It hadn't been much
of one. People just seemed to be glad that Darnley
was gone and Will recalled that the Queen had at-
tended a wedding shortly after the death of her hus-

band. Whose, he had no idea, but he did remember having to prepare the meats for a wedding feast, albeit a modest one, under the circumstance, but a celebration none the less. How could that be in order if the court was supposed to be in mourning? Later a reward of £2000 had been announced by the Privy Council for anyone who had information that could lead to the criminals. A few people had been questioned but there had been no arrests. So now, they were holding a trial for Bothwell. How could he be standing trial? Accused of what? Who was going to come forward as witnesses?

Will now knew exactly how he would be spending his free time that day. There was quite a crowd already milling around the High Street in Edinburgh when he got there. The atmosphere might even have been considered festive, drinks and pies for sale everywhere, if it had not been for the hundreds of Bothwell's supporters flocking in on every side. He recognised Bothwell's arms on display, that hare again. And Will joined the milling, listening and observing. The crowd gave him confidence, even though the mounted soldiers, the Hepburns with their family crest, were an intimidating presence. He remained silent though everyone else had plenty to say. Will always hesitated to speak in public places. There was that English accent to hide. People had turned on him in the past, blaming him for every trouble in their lives. Everyone knew the English wanted to take over Scotland, didn't they? They were thieving mischief makers, weren't they? In any case, you could learn more by listening. But even listening had to be discreet.

'Can't blame Lennox for not turning up with all these Hepburn people around.' It was someone with a loud voice standing just behind Will. He stepped away. Hepburn was Lord Bothwell's family name. His family had strength and influence in East Lothian and the borders.

'Aye, and Lennox is only allowed six attendants. That's the law.'

'Seems a bad omen to me.'

'Seems unfair too, when Bothwell has all these supporters.'

'It's only Lennox's petitioning the Queen that has got him this trial.'

'It can't be official then? The Queen's not getting involved is she?'

'She's not here. Ill again.'

'I'd be ill after all she'd had to go through.'

'Aye, and I heard a messenger arrived early this morning from the English Bess and he wasn't even admitted to see her.'

'What was the message about?'

'Now, how should I know that?'

Will heard later that the messenger had turned up in the kitchen complaining about the dismissive response to his journeying so far and so early to be sure he arrived in time to deliver his message. He had named himself as John Selby, Provost Marshal of Berwick. No-one in the kitchen knew what a Provost Marshal did, but it sounded important and they rushed to feed him. And were shocked when he said he had been turned away by the Queen's advisors. He wanted feeding and the opportunity to vent his feelings. The kitchen workers were happy to oblige ... and listen! He ranted forth, saying it was all an insult to his own Queen Bess. The man didn't know what the message was either, except that it was something to do with the trial.

Later, Will learned that it was a request for the trial to be postponed so that the Lord Lennox could gather his own supporters, and so that he could safely attend the trial for the murder of his son. His son's enemies were still at large. He claimed his own life was in danger. He also claimed he needed time to prepare an informed prosecution. Lennox was, therefore, deprived of the trial he had thought would be more fair. Even Will could see the way matters were leaning. Lennox had obviously been intimidated by all those Bothwell people. It turned out too that it had been a Hepburn man who had told the Provost, Selby, that the Queen was sleeping and could not be disturbed.

And at that very moment, when Will had been listening to the crowd speaking out, someone had pointed upwards to indicate the Queen with Mary Fleming standing at the window to watch the horsemen leave. Not so sick then that she couldn't get out of bed? Or had she been lying even, to avoid trouble? Could you accuse a Queen of lying? Will certainly wasn't going to try but he thought how furious Lord Randolph would have been at the sleight to his own Queen's messenger. There seemed to be something wrong in what was going on, even to Will's inexperienced eyes.

Will had been in the Canongate with the crowd as Bothwell came riding down with more Hepburn followers on horseback in his train. The trial was due to start at noon. Will followed the crowd as it milled towards the court room but there was such a crush to enter that even Will, skinny lad though he was, hadn't been able to slip in. Will wouldn't have recognised Bothwell except for people shouting out around him. He saw a rather stern and serious man, clean shaven but with a carefully trimmed moustache. He held himself erect as a pole on his horse and turned aside for no-one. Will could feel the arrogance of him. The crowd also shouted for two other lords riding alongside. Will recognised Sir William Maitland. His mother had once pointed the man out. She knew him because he had recently married Mary Fleming, one of the queen's Marys. Everyone knew that the Queen had four special ladies, four maids all called Mary... Mary Seton, Mary Beaton, Mary Livingston and Mary Fleming. They had all accompanied the queen to France as royal maids when she had been sent there as a 5 year old to marry the French Dauphin. They were no older than she was at the time, more playmates than maids. They had all returned with her too when the Dauphin had died. The Dauphin had become King of France when his father Henri II had been killed... a lance through his eye at a tournament. The story made everyone wince and added spice to the tournament games Will played as he grew up. Mary had been Queen of

France for no more than a year. The four Marys were obviously loyal and caring, but Randolph had called Maitland a devious, man, though he did acknowledge that he was a clever one too. Maitland had become Mary's Secretary just as he had been Mary's mother's secretary before that. He was a strong Catholic, a good enough reason for Randolph not to trust him. It seemed as if there would never be any agreement between the two religious factions. Mary of Guise, Mary's mother, had died whilst Mary was in France. That was when Lord Moray had become regent.

The other man riding alongside Bothwell was Earl Morton. Will had heard of him. He was supposed to be part of the conspiracy against Rizzio and then later against Darnley. Why wasn't he being tried? Not to mention the others whom Randolph had fingered for both crimes? Morton had sometimes come into the kitchen, though the Lords rarely did, They usually expected to be served personally in their chambers. Morton had been loud and coarse, making ribald remarks about some of the female workers and following those up with lewd gestures and actions.

There was no sign of Lord Moray, the Queen's half-brother. Randolph had suspected that Moray had been involved in the planning for the death of Rizzio and for the murder of Darnley, but the man always seemed to have the uncanny knack of somehow disappearing well before anything happened. He would argue that he had been in London or Glasgow or anywhere. He was never charged with anything but Randolph knew he was not the supportive brother Mary thought he was. Randolph had always thought she was deceived by the man's smiles and cajolery. He said that Mary was naïve in not realising that her return to Scotland had been a hindrance to Moray's ambitions. Moray wanted nothing more than his own power and everything he did seemed to serve towards that. He was a manipulative rascal but, even though Randolph called him a snake, he had to support him as he was the Queen of England's man. He was the Protestant force against the threat of the Scottish Catholics. A shifty, unpleasant man who had been the real power behind the throne until Darnley had arrived in Scotland to marry the real Scottish monarch, Moray's younger and trusting sister, Mary. Sometimes, Will felt sorry for Mary. She didn't seem to see the snakes writhing in the grass around her.

FIVE

Will was back in the kitchen in time to start cooking the meats for the evening meal. Others who had been freed up sauntered back in after him. No one had been able to get into the court room, but Gillie, the saucier, who had been working the day through and been nowhere near Edinburgh, felt emboldened enough to declare that Bothwell would not be imprisoned.

'What makes you say that?' Tom Croft, who decided most of the menus after consultation with one of the Queen's household staff, spoke for many of them. What they really wanted to say was 'how do you know that when you've been here all day?' Gillie seemed to think his position as saucier enhanced his standing in the kitchen, if not in the Palace. The others didn't. Behind his back, they said it was just because he came from Paris, but that didn't impress them. They, like most of the Scots, did not appreciate fine sauces.

'Clear as your nose,' Gillie explained. 'He

commands the Queen, therefore no one will counter him. No one would dare.'

'You may be right,' said Bessie, who organised the vegetables, 'I wouldn't want to argue with him. Remember what his page Paris said when he came in once.'

'Me neither,' said John Parlick, who had been another of the lucky ones who had been able to go into town. His job was cutting up the cooked meats and preparing them on platters for presentation. He would not be needed so much until later but, as chief cook, he was generally around to supervise the cooking. He was the person who checked that Will and Derry were turning the spit fast enough. Or slowly enough. Sometimes, the spit heights had to be altered to stop meats drying out. It was John Parlick who decided all that.

'I saw all Bothwell's supporters riding in with him in the Canongate this morning,' he said now. 'There were enough of them to put anyone in their place. Enough to intimidate any judge, no matter how guilty Bothwell might be.'

'What did Paris say about him?' It was a timid question from Jennet as, like Will, she hadn't been working in the kitchens very long and was expected to know her place in the hierarchy. Will was glad she'd asked as he hadn't been there to hear what Paris had had to say about his master either, though he did know who Paris was. Paris's real name was Nicholas Hubert and he was sometimes referred to as French Paris because that was where he was from. He'd worked for Lord Bothwell, when that Lord had been in France with the Queen, though he had moved into the Queen's service shortly before the King's death.

'That for the six years he had worked for Bothwell, he had been bullied, kicked and beaten by his master.' Bessie shook her head. 'I believe it too. Not a nice man, that Bothwell. Don't know how he has so many women. Actually, I do and it's not nice, not nice at all.'

'They probably don't have much choice either,'

John said. 'Did you hear about your namesake, Bessie? Bessie Crawford? I heard he had her locked up in a barn or some such once, and wouldn't let her out until he had had his way with her.'

Bessie said nothing audible but she was mumbling. She sounded bad-tempered.

'The Queen trusts him though,' This was Tom Croft again. 'He's loyal and stands up for her above all others. I wouldn't trust any of them myself.'

The door opened. Silence fell upon everyone and all eyes settled dutifully down upon their work. But it was only woodcutter Glennie and the atmosphere lightened again.

'Well, guess what', he announced.

'You want some pottage?'

'Well, that too, but you have to guess what happened today.'

There was silence again. They had already discussed that.

'Ah, you're no fun.' Glennie wrinkled his bulbous nose and revealed that Bothwell had been acquitted.

'Just as I said.' Gillie was pleased with himself.

'Fine,' agreed Glennie, 'but did you know that he sent the town crier around the whole of Edinburgh to announce the fact? And had placards posted to the town gates and the Tollbooth, emblazed with his arms?'

'He's a braggart,' exclaimed Bessie, back in the conversation.

'You don't like him then?' teased John Parlick.

SIX

The Queen made her first public appearance after the death of her husband, King Darnley, when she went in procession to the Tolbooth for the first day of her new parliament. The kitchen staff, along with many others, all went out to stand in the courtyard of Holyrood Palace to watch her as she left. They saw her helped gracefully on to her horse and surmised that she was wearing some kind of long, dark robe, made seemingly of velvet with lace cuffed sleeves. They could just see beyond the heavy cape which hung in folds around her and over her horse behind, to ward off the chill of the early morning.

This was the closest Will had ever come to her. He could see her slender hands clutching at the reins and her red golden hair which fell softly around her face across the horse's mane. She held herself like a Queen. She seemed to have refound the strength Will had seen in her before. It brought him a sudden surge of hope that things might turn out well after all. As Will looked on with the others, Queen Mary looked as regal as a Queen should, though Bessie, standing watching from the doorway of the kitchen, said she looked pale and tired. She certainly looked sad and was not smiling, although the people standing to watch her go were shouting out greetings and good wishes. She did not answer. Will thought that he must have seen her in Paris but he couldn't remember. He certainly couldn't remember the sombre atmosphere that prevailed in the Palace now being anything like the joyous ambiance of the French court. His memories saddened him.

She rode off, surrounded by some of her lords as well as by many arquebusiers, instead of the customary Edinburgh baillies, her government officials. The arquebusiers were armed men. Was that for show, Will wondered, or was the Queen still nervous and anxious after Lord Darnley's murder? Who could blame her? She had told everyone that she believed that she had escaped her own death twice when both Rizzio and Darnley had been murdered. She had said that a pistol had been placed against her pregnant stomach as Rizzio was being torn from her skirts and that she would have been shot except that another of the lords had pushed it away. And again she cried that she had been planning to stay overnight with Darnley the night he was murdered at Kirk o'Field. It had just been chance that she had made the last minute decision to return to the Palace and thus save herself.

As Will thought about all this now, there were so many things to consider. Oh, Darnley and some of the other lords had murdered Rizzio all right and it must have been a terrifying experience for her, especially when she had been pregnant. The kitchen people had talked of little else for days after that murder, discussing it every time a new detail came to them, being amazed that such a thing had happened almost under their noses. The Queen had been in her private room playing cards with her ladies and Rizzio. Or had he been playing his musical instruments for them to sing to? Whatever, lots of armed men had suddenly burst into the room from the staircase leading down to the King's room which was below Mary's. The men had pulled Rizzio away. It must have been so confusing and alarming in such a small room and amongst so many armed men. Rizzio had had to be torn from the Queen's skirts. He had been clinging to them to save himself, pleading that she should help him. But what could she do? Will was amazed at the daring of such an incident with the Queen in the same room. Where had the guards been?

Rizzio had been dragged away, stabbed, and left for dead at the bottom of the stairs. Rumour had it that there had been fifty-six stab wounds or more, with Darnley's dagger left sticking out of the body when it was found. Who on earth would have counted the wounds? A gruesome task, whoever it was. People said that the dagger had been left there in the King's body so that everyone would know who had led the murder, so that the Queen herself would know that her husband had been at the centre of it all. The whole palace had been in turmoil for days, nay weeks afterwards, and Will, like everyone else, did not like to think of it now as he watched the Queen ride out.

Darnley had denied the murder but the dagger was most definitely his and he had later admitted to his wife his part in the whole thing. Then he had helped Mary to escape from the scene of the murder. The two of them had ridden off in the night together to Dunbar Castle and as soon as he was safe, Darnley had dared to point fingers at everyone else who had been in the plan with him. Like most people Will considered him a lying sop. Decidedly stupid too, if he thought he could save himself by pointing fingers at everyone else. He could not understand how Mary could tolerate the man. People said she had feigned to forgive him. She had had to. It was the only way she could escape from the Palace. She had charmed Darnley with promises and, with Darnley being a man who thought only of his own interest, it had worked. The silly fool had believed her and Will re-alised now that Mary could also lie when she felt it necessary. Darnley had been trying to save his own skin just as she was trying to save hers. What a pair they were! Was it any wonder that lots of people had wanted to kill him later? All his former fellow conspirators to start with. He had betrayed them all. Not that they were worth much either, each one fighting the corner which suited him best. It was a miracle, thought Will, that Darnley had lived as long as he had after Rizzio's death.

'There's your friend,' John Parlick nudged Bessie. He was nodding towards the Lord Bothwell, who was leading the procession, carrying the royal sceptre.

'I see him,' said Bessie. 'Taking the lead in all his arrogance, as if he's the most important person there.'

'Well, for the moment, he is, isn't he? If I had all those men to follow me, I'd expect to be obeyed. And he's eliminated all the opposition for his place next to the Queen.'

'For the moment, as you say,' Bessie agreed, 'but

there are many who dislike his rough haughtiness and will come to challenge him. Eventually, the Queen will pardon those rebels hiding out in England and they'll be back with anger firing their vengeance.'

'Who are the other Lairds there?' asked Will and he pointed to two richly attired men, one carrying the royal crown and the other the official sword.

'I think the first one with the crown is Argyll, Not a man to be messed with,' Tom Croft explained. 'Far richer than Bothwell. He's the chief of the Campbell clan. Very thick with Lord Moray and married to the Queen's half-sister. Bothwell will need to watch his back.'

That must be another of the late King's bastards, thought Will. There seemed to be so many of them, but he said nothing. Everyone else seemed to think bastards of no importance, no shame to be required. It was what he was too and so he was pleased in a way. He asked about the second man.

'That's the Earl of Crawford. Loyal to the queen,

but a brute of a man.'

It all confirmed that the realm of Scotland was the uncivilised place Will had always thought it, from the first moment he had arrived. He now felt it even more. The people were uncouth and there were too many factions who fought amongst themselves and with everyone else too. They were an argumentative and rebellious lot. The weather was worse than in England and the place was generally filthy. Foulness was everywhere in the streets. Even the palace at Holyrood didn't impress him. It hardly compared to those French palaces he'd once known. Lord Randolph claimed Queen Elizabeth's courts were also far more glittering. Will didn't know. He had never been to the Elizabethan court, but the whole country didn't compare well with England according to Randolph and now that his mother was gone off with Lord Randolph, he wondered how he would be able to get out of the place. As they all trudged back to their work, he felt downcast at the idea of turning that spit for the rest of his life. He just couldn't.

SEVEN 19th April 1567

The Parliament sat for several days but Will and his fellows heard little of the proceedings except that Bothell was lawfully confirmed in his innocence over the death of the King and that certain lands were granted to him and some of his supporters.

'So, Bothwell rises even higher for doing very little and we all remain where we are for working so hard and for so little every day.' That was Bessie. Everyone else shrugged and mumbled that it was ever thus. 'Well, it shouldn't be,' she concluded and stabbed down hard on the turnip she was cutting.

Bessie was usually good natured. She was a big lady with ample bosoms and a hearty laugh, but today they had all been told they would be working late to accommodate Bothwell's wish to entertain in his private apartments. He'd sent down his requirements and was ordering a lavish feast for over thirty people, his lords and some of the prelates from Edinburgh. They assumed that he was celebrating his acquittal at the court. Bessie wasn't the only one to be disgruntled. She was tired. They all were. And they knew that Bothwell would be carousing until late into the evening. Bothwell was another lord who drank too much. The servants would be clearing up and would be late to bed. Then they would have to be up again for four in the morning as usual, whilst Bothwell and his people would all be able to lie abed until whenever they wished.

All the dishes were ready on time. John fussed over the platter arrangements whilst Will and Derry, his fellow spit worker, were told to change out of their old clothes and join the waiters in carrying the food over to Bothwell's lodging at the other side of the building. Not for the first time did Will think that this ferrying to and fro of the different courses to different places in the Palace was a silly arrangement. The food would be cold or at least luke-warm by the time the diners received it. And then all the dirty pots would have to be returned, which was an even worse job. Carrying dirty platters and bowls through long corridors meant staining one's clothes with congealed vegetable and sullying one's finger with some of Gillie's dribbling sauces. And all because the higher people felt it would be safer if the living quarters were away from the fires of the kitchens. Perhaps that did make sense? The Palace had so much wood in it.

Still tonight's dinner meant that Will did get to see Bothwell again and all the other people whose names he hardly knew, all over-dressed in their fine outfits and vying with one another in their witticisms. Will felt that there was a crudeness to some of them. It was hard to see them as his superiors. He and the other waiters were scarcely recognised as people as they moved between them. Conversations continued over them. Their very existence was ignored. However fast and carefully they worked to serve everyone fairly, it was never good enough. An impatient diner was a selfish diner. Now was the only word such a person understood. They snapped and snarled like angry dogs. It was no wonder such meals, fueled by too much wine, often ran to quarrels, if not knife fights.

Actually, Will thought that this ceasing to exist as a human being for servants could have its advantages, especially towards the end of the meal when Bothwell was calling for quiet and the last of the dishes were being cleared and the waiters dismissed. No-one would notice his lingering to the end. He was just part of the background. Will went off with the last of the servants but then paused and put his dishes down at the end of the corridor.

'I think I've left one of the carrying cloths behind,' he whispered to Derry.

Derry nodded and continued on his way. Will crept back and put his ear against the door. If he concentrated, he could hear Bothwell's voice quite clearly. As host, Bothwell had been sitting at the head of the table at the door end. The other voices were less easy to understand but it seemed to be Bothwell who was doing all the talking so that the odd missed comment didn't matter.

'You may all share my concerns that our gracious

Queen is destitute of a husband. Our land of Scotland cannot permit her to remain in this solitary state. You all know that I have been cleared of the pernicious rumours regarding the death of our noble Lord Darnley. The kingdom now needs another heir. Do we want another English man or other foreigner for the Queen's husband?'

There were some murmurings and comments which Will could not make out. He supposed the room was generally agreeing with whatever Bothwell said. People were very nearly always supportive in public. It was always a safer manoeuvre. They grumbled in private afterwards.

Then Bothwell began again. 'I do feel with you that our noble Majesty would prefer one of her native born subjects unto all foreign subjects and feel that my affectionate and hearty services to her might move her to select me as her new husband.'

Will gasped and then silenced himself as if the noise of his outburst had been loud enough for them all to hear. He stilled his beating heart, breathed deeply and put his ear to the door again. From the sounds coming from within the room, it seemed that Bothwell was sending some sort of document round the table, collecting the signatures of all those attending. Will worried that someone might now decide to leave. He tiptoed away and disappeared down the corridors with his dirty dishes as fast as he could.

Will knew what he had heard and was shocked by it. He was even more shocked that none of Bothwell's visitors had cried out against the man's plan, against the sheer audacity of it, against a man of his lowly birth wishing to marry a person of royal blood. However important Bothwell's Hepburn family was, they were not so high born that they could marry into royalty. Mary had been Queen of France, for God's sake! Bothwell was just a wealthy and intimidating lord. Will was not so innocent that he could not see what the man was up to. He was getting the Lords' approval for a proposed marriage to the Queen. He then would be able to persuade Mary into marriage by telling her he had the approval of many of her other lords and that the country needed her marriage to settle the realm. Mary would have to be exceedingly strong willed to argue against such a man. And Will knew that she certainly wasn't that. She had somehow been turned into a vulnerable and fragile woman. That hope that had resurged through him not so long ago now fell flat again.

And now, Will had to wonder what to do. There was no-one he felt it safe to tell. Yet again, he swore that he could not even write to inform Lord Randolph. He was angry about his lack of learning. He knew his numbers well enough, but that was not helpful. How could knowing his numbers help? He thought of Lord Moray. He had not been one of the visitors in the room and he knew Moray was one of Bothwell's enemies and would be glad to hear of what was going on. But Will didn't like Moray either and didn't trust him in the slightest. There was no-one to confide in. Every man he could think of seemed happy to conspire in any plot which seemed to benefit them and they would then equally happily drop any allegiance as soon as its value faded. Will was alone. He helped with the clearing up in the kitchen and then took himself off to bed. He felt scared just knowing what he'd overheard, as if his face would be a revelation of everything in his mind.

EIGHT

Will sucked long on his new knowledge and even got himself told off in the kitchen for being inattentive. It was the first time for many months that he had been found wanting and if he wanted to leave this job to make his way forward in the world, to escape to somewhere less unpleasant, it would not do. He had to prove his worth and responsibility. The criticism straightened his thoughts and in any case, nothing seemed to be happening beyond the kitchen. The Queen had left Holyrood, gone off with some of her followers to Seton. It was the place she always seemed to go to for rest and quiet. She was heard saying that she was also looking forward to seeing her baby son, James, on her way back, calling in at Stirling, which was traditionally the royal nursery of the Scottish kings. Her absence for a few days made it possible for the servants to clean the Palace properly. Those unsavoury corridors began to soak in the fragrances of lavender and rosemary again from the cleaning water.

The Palace was quiet without all the royal hangers-on. There were fewer meals to prepare. There was time for leisure and conversation. But all that came to an end when the palace and Edinburgh itself rang with alarm bells. The sound stopped people where they stood, looking at one another with dismay. It was easy, given the tension of Edinburgh and the Palace, for them all to feel as if they might be under attack. Or was it a fire? Eventually, Tom Croft drew himself up and took it upon himself to leave the kitchens to go out and investigate. Few words were spoken during his absence. Every ear was listening to see if there were noises in the corridors or outside. Tom came back, only moments later, saying there had been nothing to see.

That left them all with a restlessness that stretched until the evening when a man from the Wet Kitchen called in with a delivery of fresh fish and related what he'd heard. Even then no one was sure that what he said was true. He said that a message had been sent by the Queen to the Lord Provost, in which the citizens were begged to attempt a rescue. From what, from whom, was not clear. It was late at night and no-one rightly knew where the Queen was. There were no instructions about what to do and so everyone just continued with their work. That calmed them.

And slowly, information filtered in. Those in the kitchen felt that they were the last to know, but what did it matter that people whose only use was to cook a chicken were not informed? What could they have done if they had been told? The Queen and her retinue had been on their way back to Edinburgh after her visits to Seton and Stirling and were only a few miles from their destination when they had been intercepted by Bothwell with a huge force of men. People said at least eight hundred, but who could have counted them in the dark? Such a huge figure merely meant a lot. The story was that Bothwell had ridden forward to put his hand on the Queen's bridle. Tittle-tattle fussed that that was an insolent move on his part. He should not have dared to touch anything of hers. Bothwell had ridden out from Holyrood and had supposedly told the Queen that there was danger for her in Edinburgh and that he would take her to safety to Dunbar Castle. What danger? No-one in the kitchens knew anything about that. Her Majesty had seemed to accept Bothwell's words even though some of her followers had wanted to defend her against him. She had agreed to go with Bothwell, saying she wanted no bloodshed, though she or someone in her train, had sent that confused message to the Lord Provost which suggested that all was not quite as well as she was making out. Where had the mention of rescue come from? The citizens of the city had fallen into confusion, not knowing what they were supposed to do, or even if there was anything they actually could do. So, in fact, they did nothing and when eventually news came that her Majesty was in the castle at Dunbar with Bothwell's eight hundred men surrounding the place and all the gates of the castle firmly shut, it was actually too late to do anything. Canon shots had been fired from the Edinburgh castle as horsemen thought to be Bothwell's rode past in the distance. They were well out of range. It was a futile gesture. No-one knew the full or true story.

The tale became even more embellished in the retelling. The anxiety and confusion of the previous evening became high-handed outrage. Rumours fed upon rumours and there was a buzz of questions without answers throughout the whole of Holyrood Palace. Not everybody admired the Queen, but at the very least, she was their Queen and should be treated as such. The kitchens were no less affected.

'I knew it,' said Bessie. 'I knew that no good Bothwell would cause trouble. What's he up to now?'

Will, with his own private knowledge, thought he knew the answer. Bothwell would be working on the Queen to persuade her into an ill-advised marriage, trying to convince her that it was so counselled by all her lords. He'd be showing her that document that he had had all the lords around his table sign.

However, Will kept his ideas to himself, though he didn't need to for long. Soon, others in the city had come up with similar answers of their own and they spread to every part of the region. In the kitchens, where the extra leisure time gave them all the opportunity to think more deeply, careless comments flew through the air.

'He's wanting to marry her to further his own ambition.'

'It seems that some people knew about it in advance.'

'Who?'

'I don't know, but I heard that many of the lords have agreed that he should marry her. They signed a bond to support him.'

Will remained silent even now. He guessed that with at least thirty guests at Bothwell's dinner, it had always been likely that someone would speak out. Keeping a secret when so many people were involved was impossible. And if he said anything, might he be accused of spying? Well, it was only a sort of spying. If he didn't tell anyone what he knew, how could it be spying? Spies were paid for information. No-one had paid him. He was just guilty of curiosity.

He wondered what the Queen would be making of the incident. That there was no danger for her in Edinburgh must already have become obvious to her. She either knew Bothwell had been lying or she didn't care. Already there were rumours that she had known in advance that Bothwell was going to intercept her journey. Word was that she could only have been so calm because she had expected it, had been waiting for it. It had not been an abduction; it had just been made to look like one. It had all been planned. Bothwell had the signatures to prove it was what her people wanted. Was he asking her at this very moment to marry him? What sort of Queen was Mary turning into? Will found it hard to believe that she was scheming. He had been happier when he had trusted in her sincerity. Was this what growing up was all about, discovering what people were like? He found it hard to believe that Mary couldn't be trusted. But he remembered how she had deceived Darnley to affect an escape when she needed one after Rizzio's murder.

But how could Mary marry Bothwell? The man was already married; he had been for about 2 years now. Will remembered helping to prepare the wedding feast for the newly married couple. The bride had been a Lady something Gordon. And Mary had helped with dressing her, for an event which had been celebrated throughout the city.

And there was also the question of Bothwell's religion. He was an ardent Protestant. And there was Mary with her strong Catholic faith. Surely, she couldn't countenance marriage with a Protestant? And Bothwell was said to be so entrenched in his Protestantism that he had even refused to enter the Catholic Church when the infant Prince James had been baptised. He had stood and watched from the door. Mary had already had two husbands and both had been Catholic. The French Dauphin and Lord

Darnley had both been chosen for her because they were Catholics. And now she was supposed to be accepting a non-Catholic. Was it even possible? Outrage was fast becoming dismay amongst the populace.

It was both shameful and exciting that all this was happening under the very noses of the ordinary people at Holyrood. The gossip flowed constantly as rumour was piled upon rumour. Just when it seemed that things couldn't get any worse, it was whispered that Bothwell had raped the Queen. The whispers were soft at first from people huddled in corners. Probably because no-one could really believe it. Then when the rumours widened into apparent truth, voices became loud and vociferous as people swallowed down their indignation and began to accept all manner of wildness. What had first been outrageous was now fact. Bessie, however, had believed it all from the beginning.

'There is nothing I would not believe of that man,' she said, when everyone else was in dismay and disbelief. 'He is the devil's kin'.

'But how could he dare?

'He could dare because he has all those men of his.'

John Parlick was easily won over. 'Don't forget, I saw them when they were riding to court. He has built up even more henchmen since then. Her Majesty must have been truly afeard to let him have his way with her.'

Kitty, who made pies out of some of the meat selected from the Flesh Room, did not speak often. She listened and said those things which everyone was thinking but sometimes thought better of saying. Now she spoke quietly, as if what she was saying ought not to be spoken out loud. Will could sense the embarrassment in her. She was not as timid as people thought. She was just quiet and self-contained. She didn't speak much because her native tongue was French. She was another of the people whom Mary had brought with her from France. She chatted happily with Gillie in French and would often come to a sudden stop, mid-sentence when she realised people had quietened to listen and gawp at their babble. It wasn't that the others could understand. It was a fascination with a seeming gabble of nonsense. Kitty didn't like eyes upon her. She just concentrated on her work and produced wonderful fruit tartlets. The meat pies were more difficult for her. The Scots liked their meat more than their fruit and the French seemed to be the opposite. Perhaps it was because it was much easier to grow exciting fruit in the warner French climate? William had watched Kitty's pride as she perfected each tart until it became almost a sin to bite into it. She was much more slapdash with the meat pies. They didn't really interest her, even though they tasted every bit as good.

Kittie was speaking with confidence now.

'There are those', she said, 'who say that the Queen wanted to be taken, that she was willing to give herself.'

'I don't believe it.' Bessie wanted nothing to soften

her condemnation of Bothwell.

Kitty was insistent. 'But the Queen has always trusted him. He is her one true and dependable servant. He doesn't approve of her religion but he is always loyal. The others change their loyalty as often as they change their shirts.'

'Which isn't often enough for some people,' said Tom Croft, not realising that Kitty thought the Scots were filthy creatures in comparison to the French.

Will smiled. Perhaps Kitty was being the French romantic, believing in the passions that stirred between men and women. What if Kitty was quiet outwardly, but a passionate creature underneath? So passionate that she could understand the Queen? He looked at her with sudden interest.

'Bothwell is at least a real man, not like that dandy Darnley. The Dauphin was always sick and frail too. Perhaps the Queen has found happiness at last?'

Those remarks caused a bit of a stir. Kitty always seemed as dignified as the Queen but perhaps the two women shared a desire for sensuality which was lacking in the rough and ready wooing of the Scottish and English. And it was amusing that the first person to agree with her was Kitty's fellow French compatriot.

'Yes,' Gillie agreed. 'I have seen Bothwell's loyalty myself, but that doesn't mean she was ready to sleep with him. He is her inferior.'

'Lord Darnley was her inferior too. Her previous husband was a King, a proper king, not like Darnley, but she was fast enough to get into Darnley's bed. I heard that she didn't even wait for the papal dispensation'.

Will had spoken. He now sat there shocked at him self for his stupidity. It did not fit with his remain silent plan? He had revealed too much. But it was done and the silence of the others made him realise that they had somehow been disturbed by what he'd said.

They all looked at one another. There was not one of them who really knew what he was talking about.

Jennet saved them 'What's a papal dispensation?'

112

she asked.

Will wished he had never opened his mouth. He was putting himself where he did not want to be. The lowest of the low in the kitchen was not supposed to be knowledgeable, was not supposed to know about papal dispensations. He knew what he knew from listening to Lord Randolph. He had even sometimes had to ask questions himself about just such things. He had asked about papal dispensations when Lord Randolph had criticised the Queen for her hastiness in marrying Lord Darnley. He had first heard of them in relation to an earlier marriage by Bothwell but hadn't thought much about them then. But now, the issue of a papal dispensation seemed more meaningful. Mary hadn't waited for the papal dispensation she needed to marry Darnley. She had been so impatient to marry the man. And her a good Catholic too, thought Will. Randolph had called it unseemly.

Now he spoke slowly. 'It's when you get the Pope's permission to do something which is against

Church Law. I'm not sure how it worked with the Queen and Darnley. I think Lord Darnley's mother was the daughter of one of Tudor Henry's sisters. Whatever, it meant that her Majesty and Lord Darnley were related by blood in some way and you are not supposed to marry someone related to you. You apply to the Pope and he will give you a dispensation to marry, that means permission, if he thinks you are not too closely related to forbid it.'

There was quiet whilst they all thought about what he'd said. Tom Croft spoke first. 'So, did our Queen and Lord Darnley have to get one of these permissions?'

'Yes. And I think they did get one eventually. But the Queen was so impatient to marry that she married Darnley before it arrived.'

'So, what are you saying?' Gillie looked steadfastly at Will.

'I'm not saying anything really. It was just referring to your comment that Bothwell is the Queen's inferior. It's good that that doesn't seem to matter to her. She values people for their real worth.' He wondered if they could tell that he was squirming inside. He didn't even know if he believed what he was saying. But he had to say something.

'I think he's saying that the Queen does what she wants. She was the same with Rizzio. No-one liked him. He was a greasy flatterer. People asked her to dismiss him, but she took no notice.'

'And with Lord Darnley. Not many people wanted her to marry him, but she married him anyway. Your English Queen was against it.'

'And now she's going her own way with Bothwell.'

'But she's the Queen. Doesn't that mean she can do what she wants?'

'Not entirely. Royal people are supposed to think of their country. They have arranged marriages. They can't marry just who they fancy. What will other countries think of our Queen? She married that foul man Darnley and now she's taking up with another.'

'Not to mention that people think she had a hand in Darnley's murder.'

'And that the man she wants to marry was probably the murderer.'

'You don't know. She might have been forced to it all. I said she must have been afeard.'

Will had already put his head down and got on with turning the spit. But he did listen. And he remembered what Lord Randolph had once said of the Queen. Lord Randolph's head had never been turned by a glossy woman and Queen Mary did not escape his rather prissy moral judgement. He'd said something about the Queen being wedded to her own opinion and that he had never met a more wilful woman.

NINE

A kind of calm settled over the palace, although there was no end to all the gossip mongering. In fact, some people were quite openly and blatantly critical. Bessie was one of those. She continued to blast forth against Bothwell. And Will felt that generally there was a turning away from the Queen amongst the people. She was now more disapproved of than lauded. There was no further talk of rescue. People were beginning to think that she had connived at her abduction and some were even stepping further than that. Will felt saddened by it all, sorry for the lady with the intoxicating smile and the beautiful golden red hair.

Then it was bruited that the Lady Bothwell, Lord Bothwell's wife, had sued for divorce in the Protestant Commissary Court in Edinburgh. The surprise from that was that she had named Bessie Crawford as the woman he had committed adultery with. Everyone had expected it to be Her Majesty's name on the documents. That really would have been a shameless disgrace. Some seemed to believe that the Queen was now brazen and ready to go beyond permitted behaviour. The Presbyterians were fervent in their reproach. There was even some disappointment that it had not been her name after all. They would have then felt redeemed in their rage. The whole world might thus have learnt of the Queen's misdemeanours. In fact, it very nearly did. Rumours had apparently travelled to France, Holland, Spain, Italy. It was commonly believed by almost everyone that the Pope might excommunicate Mary for her failure to defend the Catholic Church. People were even beginning to think that such a judgement might even be fair, so great was the Queen's growing unpopularity.

But there was worse. The rumour that Lady Bothwell had also filed a suit for divorce was soon confirmed. This did much to endorse all the other rumours that were flying free. Then came a commission initiated by the Queen herself to the Catholic Bishop Hamilton for him to try the validity of the marriage on the grounds that Bothwell and his wife, Lady Jean Gordon, were within the forbidden degree of kinship. Most people scarcely understood what that gobbledegook meant. But Will did, and the kitchen folk asked him again to explain. He reminded them all of his first talk to them about papal dispensations. He knew perfectly well that a dispensation for the Bothwell marriage had been applied for at the time of their betrothal. And he knew too that it had been granted by this same Bishop Hamilton, who was being approached to say otherwise now. Or at least to agree somehow that the couple should not have married.

Will had asked Randolph about papal dispensations, just about the time that the Queen had banished Randolph for passing money over to the rebels. Jean Gordon, the wife Bothwell was now trying to cast off … or had he persuaded her to make the first move so that he could save his honour … came from a wealthy Catholic family and had wanted a Catholic ceremony. As a Catholic herself, the

Queen had originally been their fervent supporter, and had even provided some white taffeta for the bride's dress. But Bothwell had overruled both his wife and his Queen. The wedding had been Protestant. It seemed to prove that Bothwell was indeed a fervent Protestant. And it was Jean Gordon's money that had made Bothwell a wealthy man. Now that he had her money, had she served her purpose?

So it was obvious that games were being played. The dispensation had already been given. It was obvious too that all the parties in the game knew what was going on. Bishop Hamilton's help was being sought, which was decidedly odd as he'd already given his dispensation. Surely he could now speak out? Somebody ought to before they were all in this quagmire.

Will sat with his head on the spit handle, resting. He would get into trouble if he sat motionless for too long but he needed the pause to sort his brain out. He was trying to think clearly. It wasn't easy for someone who knew so little of what went on in the wider world. What exactly was going on here? The Queen would have known about the original dispensation since she was the one who had asked for it on behalf of the two betrothed. Bishop Hamilton would have known since he had granted them permission to marry. Did she know now about this latest request to the Bishop or was it Bothwell who was pushing her from behind, commanding things in her name? If Bothwell had told her what he was doing, wouldn't she have said something to counter it? Like… 'you needn't bother with the dispensation; it was done at the time of the marriage.' If Bothwell could overrule his sovereign as well as his wife, his will must indeed be a powerful thing and perhaps the Queen was under his rule in the most dangerous way? Why was he not being challenged? Perhaps the Queen knew nothing of what was going on in her name? Or perhaps Bothwell had not known about the papal dispensation? The Queen and his discarded wife might have arranged that between them and not bothered to tell him. He was not a Catholic after all. Perhaps he had made a big mistake and had now fallen into a deserved hole? He had been found out.

But what could Will do about it? Nobody else seemed to be thinking like him. Well, he hadn't heard anybody say anything. Was it that nobody cared? Or was it that people were actually scared of Lord Bothwell? Maybe they had reason to be. He had, so people said, murdered the King. That might be reason enough. If you dared to kill a king, you were probably the sort of person who would dare to do anything.

Will thought of Lord Moray, the Queen's half-brother. Lord Moray was the one person who would have dared to confront Bothwell and Mary, his sister, might even have listened to him. But, as usual the Lord Moray was away again, this time in France somewhere. And in any case, Will didn't trust Moray to do anything that wasn't serving his own interests. Moray may even have been behind Darnley's murder, orchestrating events for a distance to bring his sister down. So, for Will, that seemed to be that. If no-one else was asking questions, it certainly wasn't Will's place to do so. He would keep his silence. It was safer that way.

Will had no idea what was going on but he did have a terrible sense of foreboding. It was creeping through his imagination, coming up with lurid ideas about all the lairds around him. There was not one to be trusted. He felt extremely uncomfortable. How he wished he were not alone! How he wished he could go to his mother and Lord Randolph and be reassured that all would go well. Lord Randolph would have known what to do. Will felt uncomfortable but he also felt stupid too, because none of all this was anything to do with him. He just cooked the meat. Why should he be anxious?

TEN 6th May 1567

That evening, the guns at Edinburgh Castle fired out in a loud salute. Deafening the guns might be, but the noise was actually reassuring. Word swept round that the Queen's train had been seen in the distance and the salute was to welcome her back. Bothwell's men followed as her escort and he himself led her in with his hand on her bridle. Those watching felt that this was again an insult, as if he were bringing her in like a prisoner or a child. They all knew that she was an excellent horse woman. She had been seen riding on so many occasions, had been riding since childhood. She had ridden at lightning speed that night with Darnley, to escape from the palace after Rizzio's murder. She had no need of any man's support. Now Bothwell's action was interpreted as Bothwell attempting to keep her in line as if she might think to ride away from him.

The decision had been made that her Majesty and Lord Bothwell were going to stay at the Castle. The Palace kitchens had been making ready to resume cooking palace meals and were now told that they weren't needed. There would be no big meals at Holyrood until further notice, but they did send for the saucier. That was Gillie. Meals at the Castle were generally much plainer than those at Holyrood. After all, the kitchens there were merely catering for the rough soldiers of the Garrison. They were not thought to appreciate meat dripping with some fancy sauce. The Queen in residence meant that a little more finesse was expected.

The question everyone was thinking, but few voiced, was why was the Queen staying at the Castle when Holyrood Palace was the royal residence? Will was certainly considering the reasons. He wondered if it was because the Castle was a more secure place and could be defended in danger. It had canons and soldiers. Holyrood had no defences. But why were defences thought to be needed? Perhaps Bothwell realised that his move to marry the Queen would not be generally approved by the Scottish people? Could he be preparing for a fight? Will could feel the mutterings beginning again. With more certainty than before too.

'Send us what news you can,' the Holyrood servants shouted after Gillie as he left with the two boys to carry his special sauce pans, his whisks, his cream measures and so forth. The news he sent back with the two lads was that Bothwell had placed 200 arquebusiers outside the Queen's room and along her corridors. No-one was to be allowed to speak to her without his knowledge. So, as Bessie now announced, the Queen *was* under Bothwell's control and the next day it was confirmed that he could marry her as he chose, for it was announced that his marriage annulment had now been authorised.

Bessie became violent with her vegetable knife again when she heard that. This time she attacked the carrots. She became even more fierce when the next news, brought in by Glennie, was that Bothwell had asked for the banns for his marriage to the Queen to be proclaimed in the church of St. Giles. The onions were well-nigh massacred. Bessie looked totally distressed, her eyes wet with the tears streaming down her face. It was probably the onions, but you couldn't be sure.

'Where's your axe?' she asked Glennie with a lumpen voice when he came into the kitchen, I could do with it to teach that Bothwell his place.'

'Outside.' He replied. ' I'm not allowed to bring it into the Palace,' the woodman said. 'We common people are not allowed to bring weapons of any kind into the Palace, Bessie, and you know you don't mean it. It would get you into no end of trouble.'

Bessie didn't answer. She huffed and puffed for the rest of the day. And Will was thinking that the common people weren't allowed weapons but the lords all had them and seemingly were allowed to use them. Rizzio had been cut by so many daggers, swords and he knew not what. But when Glennie came in the next evening, he had better news for Bessie and the rest of them. The beam on his face stretched to his ears.

'The Minister at St Giles has refused to read the

banns.' He paused to look around his stunned audience. He was lapping up his moment of total attention. 'He's not convinced that the Queen wants this marriage. He thinks, like so many of us, that she is being forced into it. He wants a written order from the Queen and a declaration that she is willing.'

'Who is this Minister? I know it's not John Knox. He's been replaced. About time too. I expect he'll come back though. He always does. He's gone off before.'

'He's called John Craig, as I understand.'

'Well, he's a brave man who dares to stand up to Bothwell. May the Lord bless him.'

'It will be interesting to see what happens next.'

What happened next was that John Craig received a written order, signed by the Queen that he should read the banns. It was most definitely interesting because in addition, there was also a declaration by her that she had not been ravished nor detained in captivity. It was Glennie again who had brought this news. That smile again.

'And what did Craig say to that?'

'He still said no, that he was not convinced. He said he wanted permission from the Kirk officials before he would proclaim the banns.'

'He *is* a brave man. He will end up a dead one too, if he continues with this.'

'It's almost as if he is declaring Bothwell a liar.'

'He is a liar.' Bessie was emphatic.

Glennie also reported that the people of Edinburgh seemed agitated beyond usual. There was such an opposition to this marriage. Will wondered if the Queen even knew how her people felt, thinking that perhaps what was going on beyond the Palace might be being kept from her. After all, Bothwell had the bond which her lords had signed supporting her marriage with him. That must have convinced her that she was doing the right thing. She might be thinking that it was her duty to marry this Bothwell, whatever her private feelings. Her lords had asked her to. Perhaps she was trying to please them?

It seemed that Glennie was as bad as Will for keep

ing his ears and eyes open. How did he manage to spend so much time in the town when he was supposed to be in the forest cutting logs? The others reminded him that Glennie had a wife and bairns in Edinburgh in a tenement house just off the Canongate. His wife was probably feeding him all her gossip from the market when she did her daily shop.

The situation developed rapidly. Everyone in the kitchen looked up excitedly every time Glennie made an appearance. The excitement went on for several days, each morsel of news more tantalising than the day before. He was plied with more pottage than he could eat so that he might stay longer and feed them with gossip. They wanted all the details. A lesser man might have been tempted to expand on what he knew but they largely trusted him. After all, he was one of them, a servant, who the lords never bothered to inform about anything. Their opinions, their feelings were never valued.

But those indifferent lords couldn't stop people listening and talking and talk they did. There was talk of the possibility of an armed rising. Alarm grew on all sides when that rumour started its journey and it seemed to be confirmed when another declared that some of the lords had ridden off to their lands to raise soldiers. Names of the lords concerned made the news even more convincing. Athol had ridden north. Argyll had gone north as well and Morton had gone to Fife, Angus and Kincardineshire. Will had no idea where any of these places were, nor who most of these lairds were. Glennie's wife had also heard that several lords had been to see Her Majesty, warning her of impending disaster, telling her not to marry Bothwell.

So, Will considered, if all this were true, Mary did know of her people's views. Surely, she would come to her senses now? But it was said that she was refusing to believe the reports. Will didn't know what to think or even if he knew what this woman, the Queen, was really like. Was she so besotted with Bothwell, that she did not care about her people? Was her faith all in him? Or was she frightened of the man? Or simply doing what he commanded?

Will remembered again what Randolph had said of her when she had insisted on marrying the Lord Darnley. People had warned her then; even Queen Bess, and her government had written with guidance that she should not under any circumstance marry Darnley. But she had taken no notice. She was Queen and she would marry whomsoever she liked. And her choice was Darnley.

Was that what it was like now? Was the Queen being similarly imperious again? She had said then that the English should have naught to do with her marriage. It was none of their affair. She was stubborn then. Was she was being just as stubborn now?

Will was uneasy. He felt some sympathy for the lady but things around him were becoming menacing. He wondered again how he could get out of Scotland. How could he leave when he didn't even know which way to turn when he left Edinburgh? How far away was Berwick? Were his mother and Lord Randolph still there in any case? Where else could he go if fighting broke out? It was beginning to seem to lots of people that it might.

Everyone was waiting for what might happen next.

ELEVEN

Glennie announced that the General Assembly of the Kirk had overridden Minister John Craig when it met on May 8th. That was what happened next. Craig was ordered to proclaim her Majesty's marriage banns for the three following Sundays.

'So,' announced Bessie, an intimidating wooden spoon in her hand. She was not as fearsome as she had been when brandishing her knives, but everyone felt her rage. 'The Kirk will now do as Bothwell wants. It's not the Queen's will, it's Bothwell's. Bothwell is the Lord of all Edinburgh. Lord of all Scotland in fact.'

'Not quite,' argued Glennie and they all looked at him with eager confusion. He had come directly from the town to recount the drama to his favourite audience. They were probably only his favourites because they fed him. Later, he would go on to his other palace venues. He was the hero of the hour.

'John Craig is still not in agreement,' Glennie continued. 'He demanded that he should speak what he feels and say it before the Queen herself and Bothwell.'

'Good Lord!' exclaimed Bessie. 'I could hug him.'

'You would squash him,' someone added in an undertone. But Bessie heard anyway and sought the culprit around the room. In her frame of mind, no-one was quite sure that she didn't mean it. Glennie, however, was twice her size and ignored her.

Glennie told the tale. Craig did not get to see the Queen. That very afternoon, he was summoned before the General Assembly, where Bothwell himself did indeed seem to rule. There was a crowd gathered outside, a host of men and women who had escorted Craig from his Kirk to the Assembly Rooms, cheering him on and then waiting outside until he reappeared. Some said they might not see him return the way he had gone in, that he might be secreted out of some back entrance, charged under who knew what ruling. Not doing what Bothwell wanted probably, but nobody knew what to call that legally.

There were attempts from those listening to come

up with the missing legal term … intimidation, threatening behaviour. Glennie ignored those. His story was urgent. He couldn't hold back now.

'But Craig did come out,' Glennie said, 'and he was cheered all over again. He said he had denounced the marriage. I heard him. He declaimed forth …'I laid to Bothwell's charge, law of adultery, the ordinance of the Kirk, the law of ravishing, the suspicion of collusion between him and his wife, the sudden divorce and proclaiming within the space of four days, and last, the suspicion of the King's death, which his marriage would confirm.' Something like that, anyway.' Glennie ended.

Glennie looked around the room, perhaps for some applause but there was just silence at the daring of such words and then a general agreement that this Craig fellow was an admirable fool. It was wonderful that he had dared to speak his mind but there was an expectation that the source of that mind, his head, would be struck off into oblivion in a very short time. As a holy man, it was perhaps only the Lord

God who was protecting him now, but how long could that last?

'And what did Bothwell say?' someone shouted.

'He objected to Craig's reasoning but what Bothwell said was not to Craig's satisfaction. Craig was in full flow now. I think he must have been inspired by the crowd's support. He said 'those Councillors are so many slaves, what by flattery, what by silence, to give way to this abomination.'

'At the end', Glennie said, 'Craig's voice dropped. We had to strain to hear him. He said 'as I left the court, Bothwell told me to read the banns. He would hang me if I did not.'

'Ah,' said John Parlick, as Glennie finished speaking 'he had better read them then. The man must live. He deserves to for his brave words. Bothwell will marry her anyway.'

The kitchen had been heavily silent all the time that Glennie had been speaking. Then the noise burst like a volcano, a noise of everyone speaking at once, not one person listening to anyone else. When the excitement began to settle down, Bessie's voice still carried over all the others, as she thumped with her fists on the table calling Bothwell a range names, most of which Will had never heard before. He guessed they were Scots. He certainly understood the intent of them. When she realised that the room had hushed to everyone looking at her, she lowered her eyes as if she were trying to convince herself and everyone else that she no longer existed. She was like a child... if she couldn't see them, they could not see her. When the whole room was quiet, she looked up again.

'Well, there's the bastard once more,' she said calmly and took up her knife, cutting the vegetables neatly again as if all was right with her world.

But everyone understood that it wasn't, that a huge step forward had taken place. They weren't sure what it all meant but they knew it meant something important. It seemed that Bessie and John Craig had somehow spoken for them all. Will also felt that everything he had heard was a condemnation of

Bothwell and that the Queen had likewise contaminated herself with her actions, or indeed with her inaction. Or did she still not know what was going on in her name? Even now, Will had no real answers.

TWELVE

Edinburgh settled down to an uneasy calm but everyone could feel the tension and knew that the quiet was false. There were outbreaks of anger as news, or were they rumours, filtered out from the castle and around the town? No-one knew. It was whispered that rebel groups had been meeting in Stirling vowing to set the Queen free and defend the baby prince.

The infant prince had been taken to Stirling, away from all the upheavals in Edinburgh. Bothwell's name was not mentioned in the rebel declarations, but some people hoped that he would be thrown out as part of the defending the Queen bit. Will even heard that some of the Lords had sent a message to her Majesty to offer their aid against Bothwell. He was shocked when he later realised that some of those Lords had been amongst those he knew had signed to support Bothwell in his proposed marriage with the Queen. Information about that private dinner had leaked out everywhere now. But Bothwell can't have been too worried as it was now agreed that he and Mary would come back to live in Holy-rood. He must have felt confident enough not to need the Castle's cannons. But Will couldn't understand how the Queen did not see that the offer from her Lords to defend her against Bothwell made it clear that Bothwell was not as popular as he had made himself out to be. If he, Will, could see it, why couldn't she?

Life in the kitchens at Holyrood returned to some sort of normality and Gillie returned with his saucier equipment. They were all pleased to welcome him back. He was a Frenchman, but that was not his fault. He was, in most people's opinion, a damn sight better than those wretched English. It seemed that the kitchen staff had forgotten that Will was one of those. He was seemingly one of them now. As for Will himself, he just sat dumb, ignoring them as much as he could. They were agitated though when Gillie told them that the soldiers at the Castle were as much against Bothwell and anxious for their Queen as they were. Rumours in the Castle were that

Bothwell and Mary had been heard arguing in their private rooms and that Bothwell was so jealous, that the Queen was scarcely allowed to talk to anyone. Even the soldiers, tough as they were reputed to be, sensed that all was not well with the royal marriage.

Gillie was pleased to be back, saying that those ruffian soldiers were scarcely the people to appreciate his delicate sauces. It was almost as if he took their lack of finesse as a personal affront. Everything about Gillie was delicate. Will was fascinated by his long and slender fingers and watched him as he poured cream slowly and lovingly from a raised jug into his concoctions, murmuring softly as the mixture thickened just as he had planned, his head nodding slightly as if he was offering the sauce the respect it merited. If he hadn't known differently, he might have thought that everyone in France had such fingers. Kitty did and he loved her beautiful hands too.

Everyone talked Gillie up to date with what had happened whilst he had been away. There had been no Glennie to report to the soldiers of the guard. They received orders and were not intended to question them. There were no factions for them. They answered to whoever owned them. At the moment, it was ostensibly the Queen, though it seemed that it was really Bothwell who ruled. Will wondered how long that would last. There was talk again of civil war.

Gillie learned that although John Craig may have published the Queen and Bothwell's marriage bans, he had not remained silent. He accompanied the bans with a sermon which called upon heaven and earth to recognise that the marriage was odious and scandalous and that he condemned the best part of the realm, including his then congregation, for remaining silent as if it had their approval. Much would people gain from their fawning flattering, he told them. Then Mary herself had appeared later before Chancellor Huntley and the Lords of the Session in the Tolbooth in Edinburgh to declare that she was marrying Bothwell of her own free will. Did anyone now believe her when she claimed that she had not been held under any restraint? It had all been for her own good, she declared, and in view of Bothwell's good behaviour and long service to her in the past, she now forgave him for what might have amounted to treason without her supportive words. She made him Duke of Orkney and Lord of Shetland, and knighted four of his followers.

'So that's all right, then,' said Bessie, in a voice heavy with sarcasm, when she heard all this being reported. She called it 'claptrap.'

'The man does what he wants and then makes her forgive him publically, so that no one can attack him for it. He kills the King, Lord Darnley, but that's forgiven and then he rapes her Majesty and that's not a problem either.'

'What is this world coming to?' commented the quiet Kitty. 'Her Majesty is not respected and people feel free to criticize where they wish.'

'Why shouldn't they?' demanded Bessie,' our roy-als should rule and set an example. Now they are just doing what they please. They should expect to be criticized. The Queen is behaving like a common hussy.'

'But they are our betters.' Kitty did not want to admit that her Queen had any faults. Perhaps she was remembering the young princess she had served in France?

'Then she should behave better. Not run after some man just weeks after that very same man murdered her husband.'

Bessie's words hushed everyone. They were shocked that she dared to say such things. Kitty was more shocked than most.

When Will met up with Jennet at the end of the day and they sat together again on the tree trunk near the midden, Jennet went back to Bessies's words.

'Why does Bessie hate Bothwell so? She has nothing good to say about him.'

Will shrugged. 'I know nothing about what makes women angry with men. Women often seem to like a braggart and rough treatment. And then they suffer for it. It's common story in the world.'

He thought of his own mother. That French man who had seduced her had seemingly not been a braggart but had had soothing words and soft flattery. And women seemed to like those things too. He resolved not to get interested in women. They were beyond understanding. He could not see the fascination anyway, though he had to admit that he liked watching Kitty. Her gentleness coupled with her strong opinions somehow fascinated him. She was a strong and principled woman. Not a girl really. But watching didn't mean anything, because he liked watching Gillie making his sauces too. He thought Gillie loved his sauces as much as he would love any woman.

'Well, I'd like to know, said Jennet, 'and I also think I know who I might ask to find out.'

THIRTEEN May 1567

The marriage contract between Her Majesty the Queen and Lord Bothwell was signed on 14th May. The kitchens got to know about the event almost instantly, as the order came that there would be a wedding breakfast for them to prepare for the next morning. Everyone had been expecting that this marriage would follow on from the signing of the contract, but they had not expected such speed. There was not only Bessie shaking her head. Tom Croft came in with the menu. He made a show of reading out what was to be prepared, holding up the paper like a town crier. No-one else in the kitchens could read so that they were all impressed. Will suspected that Tom couldn't really read either. He had been told what was on the list by the chief housekeeper and just remembered everything. No one could challenge him. They were not litcrate themselves.

The items requested brought disappointment. Gillie looked in vain for the exquisite sauces he excelled at. They were not there. The dainty pastries which the Queen had established when she had come from France were not there either. That was strange as the Queen loved them. Kitty shook her head. She would have regarded it as an honour to prepare the most delicious pastries for her Majesty. The whole thing was obviously going to be a sober affair and it was, as they later understood, to be a Protestant ceremony.

Given that nearly all the workers in the kitchens were Protestants, this should have pleased them, but when preparing for royal weddings was usually such a joyous occasion, whatever the religion, the disappointment this time was on everyone's face. The work was done without laughter, without any good natured ribaldry, without happy expectations. Underneath, there was the memory of the last wedding feast they had prepared. It truly had been a feast, with delicacies imported from all parts of Scotland, from France and from England too. Now was perhaps the only time any of them had regretted the death of that foul man, Henry, Lord Darnley. Mary too had been so evidently happy then and, whatever the marriage was to become, the wedding itself had been such a festive occasion. There had been wild boar to roast and huge swans, elaborately decorated, with trumpets to fanfare them into the main hall as wondrous masterpieces.

There were no trumpets this time. There were no fanfares either. There was a serious and solemn ceremony at the parish church of the Canongate. The kitchen workers saw nothing of that. They were busy preparing those dishes which were required and setting up a long table in the main hall. They had time though to comments on the fact that the ceremony was not Catholic when the Queen was supposed to take her religion most fervently and was an ardent Catholic. Was this Bothwell's bullying again? He seemed to be more sincere in his religion than his bride was in hers. Will remembered that Lord Randolph had once said that the Catholic Church would disapprove of Mary's marriage with Darnley and their service had been a nuptial mass. How much more would they detest this one? There was even mention of excommunication.

The public had been invited to come into the palace to view the royal wedding meal. It was a long held tradition. But on this occasion those who came stood in silence watching the Queen and her new husband eat in similar silence, with Mary sitting at one end of the table and Lord Bothwell at the other. The guests were silent too. Neither the bride nor groom looked to be wearing anything which looked remotely new or luxurious. Those who saw the Queen reckoned that she wore refurbished outfits throughout the day, a gown relined and a bit of taffeta added.

Will and Derry had been called upon to help the waiters. As soon as the meats had been unloaded from the spits John Parlick came over to cut them up and display them on the serving trays. Will and Derry changed out of their cooking rags and helped to carry the dishes up to the dining area of the great hall. Will felt uncomfortable in the ceremonial garb and from the look of Derry, wriggling and twisting his neck in the itchy costume, he must have felt the same. There was no talking. The invited public looked more bored than enthusiastic about the whole thing. All the waiters could do when they weren't needed was stand in solemn stiffness and watch. And ponder, of course, Will was, as usual, good at that. Derry was probably even better since he never spoke, even in the kitchen.

Will felt that it was like witnessing a funeral meal and maybe it was, the death of a marriage before it had even started. The married couple looked strained and formal with one another, though Bothwell was curiously polite towards his bride. There seemed to be little warmth to show between the pair, though some said that was normal in royal marriages. But that was countered with the fact that this was not an arranged marriage and, therefore, some warmth ought to bubble through. Will had heard from other waiters that Bothwell's language could sometimes be decidedly coarse, much like Bessie's the other day, but riper. He was at least restrained in that respect on this occasion. Her Majesty in fact looked sad, her face set rigid in a forlorn smile, perhaps an attempt to welcome and please her guests. It didn't work. They looked as miserable as she did. It was only a guess, but Will reckoned that, once away from the audience chambers and in her private rooms, she would let that face slip and tears would flow. He was glad to get away from it all at the end of the meal. He recollected that it was scarcely three months since the death of the Queen's first husband. What a business!

The next day, Glennie reported that a new placard had been posted on the gates of Holyrood Palace, even as the newly-weds had been eating. He had had to find someone to translate it for him for it was in what he supposed was Latin. It said, his face contorting in the effort of remembering the wording, 'Mense malas maio nubere vulgus ait.' No-one knew whether he had pronounced the words correctly. No-one cared. They just wanted to know what they meant. He enjoyed the anticipation as the kitchen people, hushed and looking eagerly towards him waited to hear his translation. Glennie had had to ask someone for that as well.

'Wantons marry in the month of May.'

FOURTEEN

The next day was a Friday, a day Will always looked forward to. Fridays were always quiet since no meat was supposed to be eaten. He had no meats to roast. People were to eat only fish as a remembrance of Christ's death on Good Friday. Sometimes, a side of pork was cooked for those hearty appetites who presented themselves early in the kitchen for something to eat the next day but on this occasion there was so much left over from the wedding breakfast that there were cold meats of all kinds. Though soulless, the wedding feast had at least been generous.

Nearly all the kitchen workers were released from their tasks. Only the poor pottage makers were kept behind. They had to provide enough for the morrow and then they too could have their own time. That accounted for Jennet. Will was pleased again. He was beginning to feel that he was treating the girl badly as he found himself trying to slip away from her whenever he could these days. She was always asking questions, searching for what he thought about everything and Will didn't know anything much anymore without Lord Randolph, and he certainly didn't know what he thought about all the goings on in the palace. He would have liked Jennet to explain it all to him, but she never had any comments of interest to make. She was just too intense about everything.

John Parlick was setting out all the old meats on fresh platters to make them look more tempting when Will slipped away and out beyond the palace. He knew what he wanted to do this morning. It had been an idea that had come to him during the week, something to take him away from his usual mooching around the palace parks or the delivery areas, doing nothing in particular, trying to fill his free time. To be honest he sometimes preferred working. It was hard for him to understand his strange loneliness, the fact that he had no family, no home to go to, no roots. Everybody else seemed to have something to do when they had time off. Oh, he had friends, but no one he felt totally comfortable with. He was missing belonging to someone. Somehow it seemed shameful to be moping when the weather was so fine.

He didn't want to go into the town. That wasn't it. He wanted to avoid seeing something which might tempt him to spend his money. He wanted to save as much as he could now, with his mother's offerings at an end. But he wasn't sure about his directions and was wondering who he might ask. And then a voice caught him. It was calling his name. He spun round, wondering if Jennet had wheedled her way into having time off and had followed him. His heart began to sink. That would spoil everything. That wasn't the company he wanted. He wanted a friend, but not her. But it was Derry. A very out of breath Derry.

'I've caught up with you. You're a fast walker'.

'But why are you following me? Is there a message for me?' It flashed into his mind that there might have been a change of plan and that he was being recalled to work. He was even brusque.

'No. I just wondered if I could have your company for a while. I don't always know what to do with my free time. Stupid isn't it? But I'm so fed up of being by myself. I know it's an impertinence. You can say no if you want. But you are the one person I thought I might ask. If you are doing something private, I have no family here to visit, but you might have. I'll just go away if you want your own private time. I won't say anything to anyone.'

Will looked at the lad who was breathing more normally now. It was strange that the lad seemed to express his own anxiety. He must really have wanted to catch him. He must have run all the way from the Palace. But he couldn't think why. He was annoyed too. Derry was not his choice of a friend either. His plan for the day was shattered, and did he want to trail this usually morose fellow around with him, doing nothing in particular? Just like all his other moments of free time? Just as, for once, he actually did have a plan? He looked at Derry who was trying to smile a sort of winning smile that would make Will feel sorry for him and take him wherever he was going. With all the selfishness of youth, Will had never thought that anybody else in the kitchen might not have local family or need a friend. Derry had never behaved as if he needed company. Quite the opposite in fact.

'I know,' said Derry,' I'm not usually much fun. I wouldn't blame you, but I've watched you all this time and think we could get on well together. Just because I don't say much doesn't mean I can't think. I'll fit in with whatever you want to do and you can trust me. If I don't speak much, I won't be telling anyone your secrets, will I?

'I haven't got any secrets,' said Will.

'So, where were you going? If it's not a secret then.'

I wasn't going anywhere in particular.'

'I think you were,' argued Derry. 'I saw you set off so fast as if you had a set destination in mind. When you stopped, I think you were having to think about your route, which way to go next. Tell me where you want to go and I might be able to help.'

Will was amazed that Derry was absolutely right. It also troubled him that he could be so predictable in his movements.

'You *have* been watching me, haven't you?'

'Yes, but don't worry. I'm always watching. I watch everyone. And I've watched you so much that I sort of know you now. You watch people a lot too... I've seen that … but you've never really watched me. You probably think I'm not worth watching.'

Will ignored that. Derry perhaps was searching for reassurance and Will was not going to give him the satisfaction. 'Why do you watch people?'

'Why do you?'

'Because it's so tedious just sitting at the turnspit all day.'

'I know. That's true. But I watch to see what people are really like. People reveal themselves in all sorts of ways. I said you can trust me. I think, after watching you all this time, I can trust you too.'

Will's brain was tumbling over. Derry's conversation was a revelation. It was true that Will had never really watched him. He had dismissed his turnspit partner as little more than a tongue-tied dullard and now he seemed to have more common sense to his name than many of the others in the kitchen. Could he be trusted? Will did need a friend, a proper friend, and perhaps Derry did too. He took a great breath.

'I was just going to have a look at Kirk o' Field. You can come with me if you want.'

He had calculated that there was no harm in telling Derry. Anyone could presumably go and look at the place where Lord Darnley had died. It didn't mean anything. It was just morbid curiosity. He just hoped the lad wouldn't blab on too much and prove a nuisance. Jennet blabbed on with all her questions. Otherwise, he would have to come again some time on his own to see it properly and he was unlikely to have so much free time again from his work for a long time.

'Oh', said Derry, 'I've been there. It's not far. Follow me!'

'What did you go there for?'

'Same reason as you, I imagine. Curiosity. I wanted to see the place for myself. Obviously, I didn't discover who the murderer was, but maybe you might see more than I did.'

'Are you laughing at me?' Will was a bit offended by this young slip of a lad, who seemed to be taking the lead when Will had considered himself to be the more outgoing, more adventurous one.

'Of course not. But I saw you slip behind that time when Bothwell held his special dinner and you knew that big word that means the Pope has given people permission to marry. I knew you were trying to find out what is going on in this place, because something is, don't you think? By the way, what was that word again? I've forgotten it.'

'Dispensation. So what do *you* think is going on?'

'I don't know. That's why I thought we should get

together. If we're going to Kirk o'Field we can sit in the garden and share our ideas.'

'What garden?' Will might also have added 'and what ideas?'

'Darnley's garden, the one he died in.'

'I thought he was blown up, that whoever wanted to kill him, piled lots of gunpowder into the cellar and just blew the whole place up.'

'Well, they did; blow the house up, I mean. But that wasn't where he died. He got out of the house somehow; it could have been before or after the explosion, and he was strangled in the garden.'

Will wondered if his mouth was hanging open. He had not heard this story. Even Randolph hadn't mentioned any of it.

'How do you know all this?'

'Common knowledge, I should think.'

Will was feeling embarrassed. And useless. It wasn't common knowledge to him. Derry must have seen his confusion.

'Actually I went to Bothwell's trial,' Derry

162

explained, 'I heard it there. Bothwell said he was in bed with his wife all night. So, he couldn't have lit the gunpowder or strangled Darnley. It's probably not common knowledge actually, but known only to those who managed to get into the trial. Of course, he might have been lying.'

'Did they ask his wife to confirm it?'

'Yes. But she could lie too couldn't she?'

'I tried to get into the trial, but there was such a crowd.'

'I know,' said Derry. I saw you stuck outside. But I'm thinner than you and just slipped in behind someone's back. No-one noticed me.'

Will's confidence was ebbing away.

'How old are you?'

'Nearly fourteen. Think my birthday is sometime soon. I'm not sure. Anyway, when I saw you outside the Court House, I knew you were interested in what's going on at the Palace. I watched you for a bit longer after that and then I made my move. As you've just seen.'

Derry stopped and waved his arm around.

'Here we are. This is Kirk o' Field.'

They hadn't come far and it had not taken long. Will felt he had been there before and not even realised where he was. It must have been before the explosion. They were in a rather scruffy rough earthed lane just inside Edinburgh's town wall. Carts passing through had left hard ruts which would be mud traps in the winter, but the place was open and flat beyond and well away from the usual squalid housing which represented most of Edinburgh. There were trees, gardens and some well-kept houses. Across a sort of quadrangle, he could see the church the area was obviously named after, Saint Mary-in-the-Field. Close to, he could also see a pile of rubble which he now guessed must have been made by the explosion. He might not even have noticed it without Derry's comments.

'That was where Lord Darnley was staying before the explosion,' Derry said pointing forward. 'It was the Old Lord Provost's house. Darnley was found in the garden behind the town wall.'

Will looked along the wall. It was a wall that was wide at the bottom but which narrowed as it rose up high to a wide, flat top. There was a small gate in it just opposite the rubble but as Derry tried it, he found it was locked. It would be the way into the garden that Derry had talked about. How could they get in there and sit and talk?

'Well, actually when I came the first time, I was climbing that wall when an old woman shouted at me to come down.'

'And you did?'

Yes, it's always a good idea to obey old ladies. They can be quite ferocious. She let me in in. Not at first though. I had to talk my way out of her sending for the Watch to get me arrested. I'm only small and just a lad and I think that won her over. And the fact that I was excessively polite. It always pays to be polite when someone might be annoyed with you. I was obviously harmless and what damage could I do in a garden? I couldn't steal anything from the house, could I? It's just a load of rubble! I just said I wanted to see where the King had died. She told me she was Lord Balfour's housekeeper. He's the one who owned the Old Provost's house. She had a set of keys for the house and the gate too.'

Will smiled as he shook his head. This lad, who had so rarely talked before, had talked his way into the Old Provost Garden and managed to get into the trial when he had not. Who was the dullard now?

Derry laughed. 'I think we'll have to climb the wall this time though.'

There were good footholds. The wall was solid and well-made, but they found quite a drop at the other side. Will landed clumsily as he jumped down onto an earthen footpath at the other side, realising that the return jump would be just as bad. He would never have done this on his own. But he had climbed far faster than Derry, probably because he had been anxious to get out of sight in case they were seen and taken by someone. He'd have a bruise on his thigh in the morning but he straightened up as Derry

166

landed beside him. He was never going to admit any discomfort to this younger and skinnier lad. It was a matter of honour.

'The old lady and I sat on that seat over there,' Derry said, moving towards it, 'and she told me everything she knew about what had happened that night. She obviously didn't know everything, but what she did know was more than came out at the trial.'

Will walked stiffly over to the seat and was glad to take the weight off his leg. It was a lovely place, with the fresh softness of late spring upon it and secluded from the strident commotion of the town. He would have liked to have enjoyed the moment there a while, but he had no right to be inside the locked and private garden and felt uneasy. His eyes followed the path which encircled the garden. It looked like someone was still looking after the place. There were some old fruit trees and a bed of herbs. The roses were just beginning to bud up and there were many flowers he didn't know the names of. There was a vegetable garden with some young cabbages. Someone was evidently weeding it regularly. It was probably a gardener employed by Lord Balfour. If he had a housekeeper, why shouldn't he have a gardener, or two? Will was beginning to feel uncomfortable, quite apart from his aching thigh. He had no idea what he could say if anyone came along and caught them there, sitting on the garden seat as if they owned the place. In contrast, Derry seemed quite at ease. It made Will feel even more uncomfortable. He felt he needed to hurry him along urgently so that they could get out of there.

'Well, are you going to tell me what she said, then? The old lady you met.'

'Oh yes,' agreed Derry, dancing up from the seat.

But first you have to imagine a tremendous noise, like thunder, renting the air and wakening the whole town. About two in the morning, she said.'

'I didn't hear it and the Palace is not that far from here.'

'Neither did I, but we are workers and so exhausted

every day that we would probably sleep through everything, wouldn't we?'

Will laughed and nodded.

'My lady friend… I think she said her name was Mrs Merton… said she heard the noise and looked out of the casement straight away and saw a lot of men running up the lane. Lots of people came out of their houses because of the noise. They all saw the running men but in the darkness could make none of them out. She said her neighbour even managed to grab one of the men by his cloak as he raced past and she shouted 'traitor' at him, but the fellow managed to shake her off and follow after the others. She said the cloak felt soft like silk so the men were not just local ruffians, poor labourers or the like.

Meanwhile, there were other people drawn in by the explosion, coming from further away. They had lanterns and were in their night clothes. Mrs Merton said she'd managed to pull a shawl over her shoulders. She'd giggled in embarrassment. It was a scene of confusion, she said, and it took them a while to realise that there was a man standing unsteadily on the top of the wall we just climbed over. He was shouting for help. Turned out it was someone called Nelson.'

'Thomas Nelson?' repeated Will. 'I've heard of him. He was one of Lord Darnley's servants.'

'Yes, that was him. He was mentioned at the trial. He'd apparently been in the house but he must somehow have been thrown out by the force of the gunpowder. He was black with dust.'

'Might he have been the person who set the explosion? Perhaps it had gone off too early by mistake?'

'I doubt it,' said Derry. 'Mrs Merton said Nelson was later taken in for work by Lord Darnley's father and he wouldn't have employed someone who had possibly been involved in murdering his son, would he? May I go on? Stop interrupting. Now, everyone knew the king had been staying at the house that night and so everyone who could, fell to searching through the rubble. Remember it was dark and cold and it was apparently even trying to snow. It must have been hard work. Eventually three dead bodies were found and there were two wounded servants who had been sleeping alongside Nelson in the gallery which gave onto the wall. That's how Nelson found himself on the wall. He was blown onto it. The other two missed the wall but survived anyway.'

'I didn't know so many people had been killed. I thought it had just been Lord Darnley'

'Well, they were just commoners, servants. No one cares much about them, I mean us, do they? They don't care about the likes of you and me. They, we, are just forgotten about.'

Both boys bowed their heads. The king had been mourned by the court, if not greatly, but at least he had had a royal funeral. The other deaths had been forgotten almost at once, except perhaps by their families. They had not even been reported. Will wondered if this would be his fate one day. He had no family here in Edinburgh. Who would care about him? And who did Derry belong to if he had no family here? It occurred to him that Gillie and

Kitty must be in the same position, having come from France. They had probably left families behind.

'There was still no sign of the King,' said Derry, beginning again, 'until someone thought to look in the garden and orchard. And there they were; they were here where we are now, the King lying not far from the house, with his valet, a man called Taylor. I can name him because he was mentioned as well at the trial. They were both nearly naked in their night clothes and there wasn't a mark on them.'

Will's eyes widened. He seemed to have missed so much by not getting into that trial. But why had these details not spread through the city anyway? Perhaps Glennie's wife had not gone to market that day? But that was silly. He had just missed hearing it. That was all.

'So how did the King die, then?'

'Well, there were no explosion marks, no broken bones, no bloody wounds, no strangulations marks but that is what was thought in the end; that they had both been strangled by someone who was skilled in these black deeds and knew how to avoid leaving marks. Or he could have been suffocated. That wouldn't leave marks either would it?'

'I don't know. I've never tried to murder anyone! Is all that possible? And who could it be?'

Derry shrugged. 'Who knows and no one has pointed a finger, except at Bothwell, who as we know, claimed to be in his bed with his wife. She is supposedly his alibi. If everyone heard the explosion, how come he never got out of bed to investigate? He was High Sheriff of Edinburgh at the time. It was his job to investigate all the crimes committed in the city. All he did was send some of his men to see what was going on. As if explosions were everyday things.'

'Or he knew already what it was because he had had a part in organising it? And didn't want to get involved from the onset?'

'Maybe,' said Derry, but there's more, the best yet.'

'More?'

'Well, Darnley was lying under a pear tree. Perhaps that one there'.

Derry went and gave the chosen tree trunk a little pat as if the thing had also suffered in the explosion.

'He'd been laid out on his back and for modesty's sake some-one had draped his hand over his bare genitals. I should hope so too. Not a pleasant thing to see, eh? Taylor, the valet was not far away, lying face down with his night shirt ridden up to show his naked rear. Then, next to the bodies were several strange things ... a chair, a piece of rope, something that could have been a bed quilt or a cloak, and lastly a dagger. Darnley had his furry nightgown and nearby was a single velvet slipper. You see what I 'mean by strange. A single slipper. And a chair. And what was the chair for? I'll let you think about that one.'

Just at that moment, the door in the wall to the orchard rattled. Someone was trying to get in. Both lads leapt to their feet and stood there for a moment, frozen. Then there was quiet. But the handle rattled again a moment later as the person tried a second time. The door still held. Whoever it was didn't have a key.

'Perhaps we should go?' suggested Will. 'They may not have a key but they may go and get one.'

'Well, have you seen everything you wanted to see?'

'I didn't know what I wanted to see. I just wanted to come. Have I missed anything? What else should I look at?'

'I didn't wander around when I came. The woman was watching me all the time. Perhaps we could just have a quick look just in case there is anything.'

There wasn't anything. Will pointed to the far wall and they climbed back from there, just in case the person they'd heard was still in the lane. Jumping down was easier this time as the landing was over-grown grass. They paused to look out from the top of the wall. They could see the mass of the city beyond. Even from a distance Edinburgh didn't look very inviting. The walk back was countrified with few people about. Will found the walking trouble-some but he kept the discomfort of his thigh hidden. He was not going to admit any deficiencies to Derry whose former reticence was totally gone. As the city drew nearer, you could almost smell it. It was the smoke from so many fires, mixed with the general smell of unwashed humanity, the detritus of over-crowding and lack of clean water. You got used to it when you were there all the time, but after being away for even a short time, the odours began to find their way again up into your nose.

'Well,' began Derry, 'what did you think about the chair?'

'Maybe it was there all the time? What kind of chair was it?''

'I've no idea. But there are benches for sitting on. You saw them. We even sat on one. And anyway, an elaborate chair would spoil in the rain. It was Febru-ary and there was snow. You wouldn't be sitting out for fun then surely?'

Will had to admit that. But he couldn't think of any

other reason for it being there. He looked at the grinning Derry, whose superiority smiled all over his face.

'You obviously think you know the answer. Come on, then, tell!'

'Well, I don't know for sure but I've had longer to think about it than you. And I went to the trial, didn't I? It was discussed there. Think about why they might have needed a rope.'

'I've thought about it; I thought that perhaps the two men could have let themselves down on the chair with the rope as they tried to escape. Or the servant let Darnley down because he was too frightened to jump. He had been ill, hadn't he? He might still have been too weak. But you said there was a piece of rope. You didn't say it was attached to the chair. They surely wouldn't have had time to untie it, would they? They'd be rushing off to escape.'

'That's a thought; I never thought of that.'

'Was that not mentioned at the trial?'

I don't think so. It was an exceedingly hasty trial. I

think the sole purpose was to find Bothwell innocent. They didn't seem to be concerned about much
else. Bothwell certainly wasn't and Darnley had no-
one to represent him. There were few questions.'

'Not even about that missing slipper? Just the one.
Whose slipper was it? That could have been the
murderer's. Couldn't it have been matched up with
someone if it wasn't Darnley's.'

'How do you know it wasn't Darnley's?'

'Because he had been escaping from his bed. Do
you wear slippers in bed? He didn't have time to put
his cloak on properly. He must have just grabbed it
and run.'

'Well, as a matter of fact, the slipper was referred
to. It was alleged to have belonged to Archibald
Douglas, whoever he is. But he denied it.'

'You didn't find out who this Douglas fellow is?'

'I think he's a follower of Bothwell's. The family
has a house just near Kirk o'Field.'

'Well, he would deny it wouldn't he? If he'd
agreed it was his, it would have been just like a con-

fession. I can't believe everyone just accepted his denial. Sounds to me that he was in the thick of it all.'

'But he was related to Darnley. Darnley's mother is a Douglas. Why would he want to kill a relative?'

Will shook his head in exasperation. 'Who knows? All these relationships are unbelievable. These lords seem to do nothing but fight amongst themselves and kill one another. It doesn't seem to matter if they are related. Then, they are pardoned a few months later. Or they make friends over something else. Make agreements, break them. It doesn't seem to matter.'

'Yes, I suppose you're right. And then they come back from banishment and start all over again. Perhaps the gangs are rearranged in between. Darnley and this Douglas chap were friends originally. I heard an Archibald Douglas was part of the band which helped Darnley in the murder of Rizzio. Then Darnley betrayed the whole band and they were all forced to flee. Later they were pardoned, just as you say, and Douglas turned to supporting Bothwell against Darnley. The murder could have been his revenge for that. At least, that's what people were saying as they came out of the trial. '

'They're all mad, Will declared. 'This is a dangerous place to live. Everybody is fighting everybody else. If I were the Queen, I'd go back to France. It must be safer there.'

Will was slowly noticing that Derry's voice was becoming more and more subdued the nearer they got to the city. He was noticeably reverting back to the-know-nothing,-say-nothing person he had been before.

'Who knows?' said Derry. 'I've never been to France.'

Will decided it was safer to say nothing too. Those unseen ears might be listening again. But he looked at his new friend and smiled. He hoped they would meet up to talk again. If he could trust him. Will still knew nothing about him. Where had he come from and how did he know so much? It can't just have been the watching. It can't just have been the old lady. It can't just have been the trial.

FIFTEEN

Derry settled back down onto the stool underneath the kitchen mantel. Part of him was glad to be back, safe in his turnspit place, but there was a sadness that the day was over and gone. He had enjoyed the afternoon out with Will but he didn't think it could happen again. It was always dangerous to make friends with people. You never knew if you could rely on them. Even with all his people-watching, most of them always ended up surprising you. You thought you knew them and then they let you down.

Will would probably not be any different. After all, what did he know about the lad? He'd admitted that he didn't have any family in Edinburgh, although Derry seemed to recall seeing him meeting up with some woman when he'd first come to work in the kitchen. He'd watched them across the great hall. Who could she have been? His mother, his aunt, his sister, a lover? No, not that last. The woman was too old for Will and Will not the experienced type who could have overcome the age difference with flattery and coaxing. But Will hadn't met up with her for a long time now. The woman seemed to be gone. And it was also strange that Will knew about things like papal dispensations and yet he hadn't said just how he knew, when Derry had hinted that he'd like to know. Even the older people in the kitchen hadn't known what dispensations were. Yes, there was certainly something on the dark side about him. But then, Derry admitted to hiding things about himself too. Why else would he not talk to anyone much in the kitchen? He did his job and kept himself to himself because he was happier that way. Anyone he opened up to was likely to disappear, leave him or just be unreliable and unworthy. That was what had happened all through his life and he wasn't going to let it happen again.

Derry's eyes began to water as he thought of those lost people now. He didn't want to. He put his head down and made out he was tired. He had been fighting hard to forget them all so that they couldn't hurt him anymore. But they refused to leave him. He could barely remember some of them; he had been too young when they had disappeared from his life, but he knew about them all. He even remembered some of them. People had told him in the past. About his mother, his father and then there was his brother, and later his sister.

First, there was his mother. He couldn't criticise her. She had died giving birth to him. But he could feel guilty and his father often made sure that he did. When life was hard, as it often was, when there was no money for food, when they had all had to go to bed hungry, that was when his father would lament the loss of his wife. Not so much because of his affection for her, but because she had been a money earner. She had worked at so many jobs, run errands for people, washed their clothes, sewed them as well. She had sacrificed herself to make sure there was food on the table for the rest of the family. She had gone without eating so that the others could. And through all that, she had had to fight his father when he wanted to take some of that hard earned money to spend on ale. He usually got his money because he resorted to his fists to make sure he did. And on his drunken return, he would wax maudlin and say it wouldn't happen again. But it always did. Derry knew all this because his siblings had told him. And the family had nowhere to go, nowhere to hide from this man who made their lives miserable. because anyone who might have helped had died before them. They also told him that his mother might have survived his birth if she had been strong-er and well-nourished in the first place; and if they had been able to afford a doctor; or even a midwife. They told Derry that it wasn't his fault. He only half believed them. And the pity of it was that there was no way he could remember her except through his brother and sister. His memory of her was empty. He had never known her.

Derry's father hadn't lasted long after his wife's death. He soon tired of coming home to no food, an untidy, dirty even, home. And to children who ex-pected him to provide, which seemed to be the one thing he could never do. Did he even want to? He kept repeating that he was looking for more work but he eventually lost the only job he had, for being drunk. And yet, he somehow always seemed to have money enough for his alcohol. And then there was the night when he came home and said he had been offered a quarrying job somewhere the other side of Edinburgh. Perhaps he had, but he went off the next morning and the family never saw him again. The children didn't make much effort to search for him. Life was actually quieter without him.

Derry's brother Jed tried hard to look after what was left of the family. When he went looking for his father at the quarry he was supposed to be working at, the people there had never heard of him. But they did offer Jed a job, though physically he was not the stuff of a quarrying man. He was a young slip of a lad like Derry himself, but he fought to do the work and did bring some money home. In the end, Jed had to leave home too as the work and the long walk to and from the quarry each day was wearing him out.

Eventually, the job destroyed him completely when there was a landslide which came flowing down the quarry side one afternoon, burying Jed and several of his fellow workers under its downwards surge. It had been raining so hard the weeks before and the weight of the rain had pulled the slope away. Derry didn't like to think of it. He saw Jed struggling as he lost his balance and then his breath. He imagined one last arm struggling as he disappeared completely. And then silence. The picture haunted him.

That left Derry and his sister Megs alone together. They had no money to bury their brother and so he went into a communal grave somewhere; they were never told where. Derry was six and Megs not much older. Derry, when he thought back to those days, thought she must have been about ten. They could no longer afford the room they had occupied with the rest of the family but managed to contrive a sort of den for themselves under the stairwell of the house they were already living in. The landlord even charged them a rent for that. It was at least dry and warmer than being out on the street and they could just about stretch out together at night. After a while, that didn't even matter as Megs stopped sleeping there. She didn't come home until the morning and Derry wondered at first, in his innocence, where she was.

Derry found out the truth slowly as for a long time Megs lied out her shame. She had been selling herself. She had discovered that prostitution paid a lot better than nearly all the other jobs open to her. She was young and her very youth attracted some of the older men who could afford to pay more for that. They were largely respectable men too, with pleasantly comfortable incomes and even more pleasantly comfortable homes, where their distinguished and well-dressed wives looked after all their other needs. Just not the particular physical needs which Megs was expected to supply on demand.

Derry didn't blame her. When he found out what she was doing, he understood that it was her way of looking after him. He didn't ask her what she had to do to get her money, but he often saw the blood on her legs, the discomfort when she sat down and the bruises on her cheeks when some of her customers had declined to pay what they owed. He tried to help in his own small way. He begged, he stole, he learnt to pick pockets and managed to keep himself safe because his legs were fast.

The two of them, brother and sister, went on like that for several years. Derry might even have said he was happy. He couldn't say whether Megs had felt the same but at least they had enough to eat. But Meg's youthful glow was fading. It had been her childlike appearance that had been her principal attraction to so many of the men who paid for her. Without her girlishness, the prices she could command began to flag. And then one evening, Megs came home crying. She had been raped. Roughly, crudely and she had been unable to clean herself up after the attack. Derry somehow understood that she usually did something with vinegar which she believed prevented her from getting with child. Life was as expectedly cruel as it had always been and, in spite of all her precautions, pregnancy was the result, though it may not have been the rapist who was responsible. In any case, there was nothing Megs could do. As the baby grew within her, Megs became increasingly unable to work at all. Nobody wanted a woman bulging at the waist and looking as down trodden as she now did. Derry tried to look after them both, but he struggled.

Derry did as his mother had done. He went without food so that Megs could have what he managed to provide. He increased his pickpocketing activities but feared that he might be caught after one particularly risky event when he was nearly taken by an elderly gentleman who looked feeble enough for him to run away from. But the man had a dog loitering nearby, just hidden in a shop doorway, which came snarling after Derry when his owner shouted his name. Derry only managed to save himself because he climbed up the outside of a house and across into an open window. From there, he was able to get out from a rear exit and leave the dog grinding its teeth and leaping as high as it could reach back in the street.

Frightened, Derry took to hanging around the Palace at Holyrood. He knew where the middens were. Sometimes things had been thrown out that he could sell. An old comb with teeth missing. They ate for two days when he sold that. It wasn't silver but it was trying to be. An old hat with a broken feather. Discoloured, but someone bought it. Sometimes, he picked at the food waste and came across pieces of rancid looking piece of meat or discoloured vegetables. However distasteful they were, it meant he could cook something to add to a few bits of stale bread to make his offerings more appetising. He expected to be sick after some of the things he and Megs ate, but their stomachs must have become hardened and they rarely were.

But if Meg's stomach had become hardened, the rest of her body evidently had not, for when her baby showed that it was preparing to come, it was too early and too fast. Derry had no idea what to do and Megs was scarcely any more informed, and when her pains began, she was not even able to talk through them to guide her brother in helping her. He went for water, shouted urgently for aid on the street, but people just walked past, their noses up in the air. He tried to give Meg sips of the water but she shook them away, tossing her head in some kind of frenzy. He added his own shabby blanket to hers and set his old coat aside to wrap the baby in when it arrived. There was no money for a nurse or a doctor but he did think that when it had been born, he might be able to take the child to the foundling hospital and get someone to take it in. It would be better off there for the moment. If Megs wanted to keep the baby, they could perhaps reclaim it later, though he thought it might have a better life at the hospital than suffering in the life he and Megs lived. He planned to leave the child on the doorstep outside so that he couldn't be grilled and reported to the police. He would need to get back to his sister.

Meanwhile, he stayed with her and held her hand, wincing when she clung to him so tightly that her nails bit into his skin and punctured it. Derry didn't know how long he had sat with Megs but after a while, it seemed that she was calming and then sleeping. There was no sign of the baby coming now either. He didn't understand until Meg's body began to go cold and he realised there was something very wrong. He put his ear close to her mouth and could neither hear nor feel anything. There was no rise and fall to her chest. He had no sense of panic. He just knew now that Megs had left him. And he understood straight away that the baby could not live without the mother. He felt that these two deaths were his fault too. Everything that had killed his mother had now killed his sister and her child… lack of decent food, the warmth of a good home, lack of medical attention, overwork. It seemed to him then that this would go on from generation to generation. How could he stop it? And he realised too that he was on his own from that moment on. He didn't move. He put his arms around his sister and hugged her. He tried to do the same for the unborn child. He was saying goodbye to them both and when he sat up, he felt tears trickling silently down his cheeks. He wiped them away with his sleeves and sat beside them both, long into the night until he was found with them the next morning. Someone took his sister away and left him there under the stairs. There was no one to console him. The sad corpse with its dead child went into another communal grave and, completely alone now, Derry never knew where that was either.

SIXTEEN

It was strange how Will and Derry slipped back to the relationship they had had before. Well, they hadn't really had a relationship, they had just worked opposite one another and Derry had been dull and silent. And boring! But just as Will was feeling happy that he had found a friend, he soon found out how mistaken that belief was. How could Will have got the lad so wrong?

All the friendliness they had shared that day when they had visited Kirk o'Field together came to a sudden stop. Once they started working again, there was no communication between them. Will was astonished. What had happened? He had joined Derry at the other end of the turnspit and made some happy quip about their afternoon together and Derry had ignored him. He had turned his head away and behaved as if Will was not even there. It was as if the afternoon at Kirk o'Field had never been. Will didn't understand. He was hurt and disappointed. He tried a few more times to start up the friendship again, but it became obvious that Derry didn't want to know. He concluded that there must be something wrong with the lad and left him to it.

After his afternoon out at Kirk o'Field, Will found it hard to sit still and largely lifeless, just turning his spit handle in his previous mechanical way, when his brain was busy churning and agitating over all he had learned at Kirk o'Field. He wondered if Derry's brain was ticking away excitedly too. It didn't look as if it was and Will had decided not to try again with someone who was so decidedly unfriendly. He didn't even see Derry in the Great Hall in the evening. Where did the lad go?

Will's brain was busy going over everything he had learned at Kirk o'Field and everything he hadn't. There were huge gaps in his knowledge. He wanted to know how Darnley had come to be at Kirk o'Field in the first place. Why hadn't he returned to Holyrood after his visit to Glasgow? Holyrood was his royal home. That would have been the more natural place for him to come back to. Why hadn't he?

And why had he gone to Glasgow in the first place?

Will knew that Darnley had been ill and he knew too about the rumours that it had been syphilis. He'd heard that Darnley had had to wear a veil to hide the ravages of syphilis on his face. Were there warts, abscesses, weeping sores? Will, in his innocence, had no idea, but he'd heard something of the sort. But was that it? Had Darnley gone to Glasgow to hide his face from the court? Was he ashamed to be seen with all his disfigurements? That would fit in with his general arrogance. He couldn't face people feeling sorry for him. His father was in Glasgow and would be there to care for him. All that made sense and, in any case, Darnley was not exactly a popular man at the court. He was known to have been involved in the murder of Rizzio and then he had betrayed those very men he had been involved with in the deed. They would be out to get him for that. They would want their revenge. But they had fled into exile and Darnley was somehow pardoned. That would be another reason why he had gone to

Glasgow. Those enemies would be back soon. He'd be safer there with his father and his father's liege-men to protect him. Then, he came back to Edin-burgh when he was nearly better. But, once again, why not to Holyrood? Had the Queen and Darnley really been reconciled? How could she think of again becoming a true wife to such a man? Will's brain shrivelled at the very idea. Surely his behav-iour with other women, with men even, not to men-tion his part in putting her through the terrifying or-deal of Rizzio's murder when she was pregnant and she and her baby at risk, would be enough to put any women off a man? Will was coming round to the idea that she could not face living with such a hus-band again. Surely she couldn't? That's why Darn-ley was at Kirk o'Field and not at Holyrood Palace. And wasn't it significant that he should be murdered just as he was on the point of returning to her at Holyrood the next day? But was she actually part of the plot to murder him? The answer was becoming more obvious.

Will would have liked someone to discuss all this with. He looked sadly across to where Derry sat but Derry seemed to be as indifferent as everyone else. They all had work to do and just got on with it. Now that the marriage between the Queen and Bothwell had taken place, perhaps they thought that was an end to everything. Life would settle down again. If there were still rumblings of discontent in the city, it was nothing to do with the kitchen people. Will found he missed all the carryings on. Perhaps it was because he had lived all his previous life alongside a man who had always been involved in such things. It wasn't just his mother he missed.

But then the whole kitchen was turned upside down one afternoon when two officers of the Palace came through the door and stood there looking around the room with ominous menace as a hush descended and everyone turned to look at them. The men had not come to get warm or wheedle some food out of the cooks. That much was obvious. The moment was tense. Everyone could feel the unpleasantness of their gaze as they took their time appraising the whole room with scowls. There were no smiles. No-one moved. Knives, spoons, pans were held aloft, suspended in mid-air, the owners waiting for what would happen next. Then, Gillie yelped as one of his sauces began to over thicken and stick to the bottom of the pan. He would have to do it all again. His yelp seemed to bring the room back to life. The two men must have known that they had to speak.

'We're looking for a woman called Bessie,' one of the officers finally said. 'Is she here?'

The silence began again. No-one was going to answer and they tried not to look in Bessie's direction to reveal her identity. But it was Bessie herself, who put her knife down to rest on her chopping board, took a deep breath, and spoke.

'That would be me.' Her voice sounded calm and controlled. They all looked towards her now. Every other face seemed calm and controlled in sympathy. But there was shock too. She took a step forward and wiped her hands.

'You're wanted for questioning.'

Everyone expected Bessie to argue, to demand why she had to go with them, to say that she hadn't done anything wrong. She was that sort of person. She would usually speak without thinking and argue black was white. But she stood quietly now and just wiped her hands. She wiped them and she wiped them, as if she'd forgotten what she was doing. Then she put the cloth down and her hands by her side and moved towards the door. Everyone else put their own kitchen tools down and seemed to be wondering about moving forward themselves. The moment held and then it was Kitty who actually did move. She went towards Bessie and took Bessie's fat and podgy hands in hers and kissed Bessie's cheek. No-one but Bessie could hear what Kitty whispered in her ear, but they saw Kitty's lips moving. Bessie just nodded. Then one of the officers tugged at Bessie's shoulder and led her from the room. The door closed behind them and there was silence again.

But not for long. When everyone began to breathe once more, there was a tumult of voices. It was hard to distinguish what each person was saying.

'What on earth…?'

'Why have they taken her?'

'Oh, poor Bessie.'

'What has she done wrong?'

'They'll be asking her questions?'

'About what?'

'About why she hates Bothwell so much.'

Will heard that last comment but wasn't sure who had made it. It was exactly what Jennet had asked him some time ago. Why did Bessie hate Bothwell so much? She has said that she knew how to find out? Who had she been referring to? Tom must have heard this more recent comment now.

'I know', he said. That quietened everybody. Everyone turned to look at him. He looked as if he wished he'd not said anything, but it was too late. He knew he was going to have to explain.

'It was fairly obvious that Bessie didn't like

Bothwell. She was always saying things about him. Like the rest of us really; we all disliked him, but she was much more intense about it. You all know that. You heard her. Well, I thought it was a bit dangerous. She was too outspoken. You can sense the atmosphere in the Palace. It's all getting tense and who knows how things are going to develop? There's things going on we don't know about and the things we do know about are pretty nasty and unsafe. There are people about who are quite happy to report others for a bit of money or a favour. I took Bessie aside one day and warned her to not be so open about her hatred. I was worried for her. You might have noticed how she's been much quieter recently. She listened to me. I didn't ask her to tell me why she hated Bothwell but she told me anyway.'

'Well?' said Jennet. Will wondered if she knew anyway and was just playing some sort of game. But she seemed to be speaking for everyone. No-one was going to let the matter rest there. It was quite obvious that Tom was going to have say more. 'Are you going to tell us?'

'Bessie began to cry. She admitted she hated Bothwell. She said she had good cause. Do you remember that one of you once mentioned a story that Bothwell had locked a girl in a barn and kept her there until he had had his way with her?'

'It was me,' John Parlick said. 'I knew the story. I told you it. It was true as far as I knew. The girl was called Bessie Craddock but that's not our Bessie. I didn't know there was any connection, otherwise I wouldn't have told you the tale.'

'No, it wasn't our Bessie', agreed Tom, but it was her cousin. Both girls were named after an Elizabeth, Bessie Craddock's mother and our Bessie's Aunt. Bessie Craddock was slim and pretty, not like our Bessie. I don't want to speak ill of her, but we would all have to agree that our Bessie is a bit too plump. But she's exactly that, she's *our* Bessie. She wouldn't be the same girl without that. Anyway, these two girls were very close, apparently. Probably because they had been brought up together? Well, when Bothwell had satisfied himself with the other Bessie Craddock, he abandoned her. It was just a moment of pleasure for him.'

'A moment of power,' said Kitty. 'He had to dominate her. He had to have what he wanted. She couldn't refuse. Some men are like that.' It was a surprising comment to come from the reserved girl Kitty usually was.

'Don't you start,' said Tom. 'I'll be having to warn you next.'

They all laughed, but it was an uncomfortable laugh. Tom began again

'Bessie Craddock, the cousin, the pretty one, was due to be hand-fasted not long after the barn incident, but her proposed partner renounced her and did not want to marry her. He said she was sullied. The poor girl was heartbroken and tried to kill herself. They found her just in time.'

'It happens more than we realise,' John said. 'What is it with some people? How was it the girl's fault?

It was Bothwell's fault. How can you blame the girl?'

No-one said anything. The room filled with silence. The silence stretched until John continued.

'Anyway, our Bessie didn't say anything because the rape and the attempted suicide could be considered shameful to her and her family. Other people might think she's sullied too. We mustn't let her know that we know.'

'*If* she comes back,' said Jennet.

'She better had.' The quiet Kitty was again showing her solid side. 'It was not Bessie Craddock's fault. The rape and suicide ought to be laid at both men's doors... Bothwell, for one moment of totally selfish pleasure and the poor girl's lover for his equally selfish rejection. Men, they are spineless. Are there any decent men around here?'

'Think on what has just happened to Bessie,' said Will. He could not help himself. 'Someone must have heard the things she has been saying about Bothwell and reported her. It could be someone here but I expect she speaks in just the same way wherever she is. Whatever we think, we must be more careful. Keep quiet, Kitty. Tom gives good advice.'

'But sometimes someone has to speak out.' Kitty was still indignant and rebellious.' If no-one speaks, it allows the wrong doers to get away with things.'

Yes,' agreed Will, 'but just for the moment, you must be silent. We'd be better off thinking how we can help Bessie.'

'Where will they have taken her?'

'I don't know. Probably to Bothwell's rooms. Or to his henchmen's. I didn't recognise either of the two men who came for her.'

'I know where Bothwell's rooms are,' said Will. 'He held that dinner there that time, when Derry and I were waiters, but I don't know who the henchman are.'

'He has so many,' said John. 'Might they have taken her to the Palace dungeons?'

'Are there dungeons here?' asked Will. It was news to him.

'Don't be daft,' said Tom. 'There are dungeons at the Castle but our Bessie is not such a danger to them that they need to take her there. They surely know that. They'll probably just ask her a few questions, warn her to keep her tongue to herself in future and then let her go.'

'I know the names of some of Bothwell's henchmen,' said Gillie. 'I heard mention of men who worked directly for Bothwell when I was at the castle. Some of those men there are not so bad, you know. They had things to say about the Lords who came and bellowed at them sometimes. There was quite a lot of spitting at some names.'

'So who?' asked Tom.

'Oh I can't remember all the names. One was a Hepburn, John, I think. There was a William Powrie and someone called Pat Wilson. Oh, and two men with the same family name, Black Ormiston and Hob Ormiston.'

'Look,' said Tom, 'I don't think we should go charging off now. This could be more dangerous than we realise. We could even make things worse for Bessie. Let's see what happens. We'll look stupid if it's nothing to do with our fears. We'll leave it for now and see if she turns up in the morning. If she doesn't, we'll think again.'

Will was thinking already. He felt instinctively that if Bessie had been reported for her words about Bothwell, it must have been someone there in the kitchen with them. He knew that Bessie usually just went straight home after her work. She lived not far from Glennie in another of the Canongate upper tenements. She didn't mix in the great hall at night. It was her family that took up the rest of her time and surely *they* wouldn't have betrayed her? They would feel like her about Bothwell. It *must* have been someone who worked in the kitchen here. Where else would she be ranting forth about Bothwell? Will moved the spit handle with slow deliberation and, without being obvious, tried to study each person in turn.

SEVENTEEN

Will woke in the morning, no wiser than when he had gone to bed. He was going to be falling into the hay and setting himself on fire like that other lad, if he didn't get a good night's sleep soon. And why did he let all these ideas worry him? Why couldn't he just get on with turning the spit like he was supposed to and leave all the pondering to everyone else? Apart from his liking for Bessie, it was really none of his business.

He had lain awake, considering every person from the kitchen as a possible informer. In the end he had decided that he knew so little about them all, that any one of them could be the squealer. He only knew that it wasn't him. He had suspected Derry at first. The lad had never spoken, had seemed evasive right from the beginning and had admitted that he watched everyone all the time. But then he had later been so friendly and open about everything he knew about Kirk o'Field. Yet, how easily he had slipped back into his original role when they returned to the

Palace. Surely that was suspicious? He was playing a double role. And very effectively too.

Minnie, he dismissed as a tongue tied nonentity, perfectly harmless, and nice enough. But weren't such people the most likely to be deceiving you behind your back? They seemed quiet, docile and innocent, and then stabbed you when you weren't looking? But really, she was just a young girl who got on with her vegetable chopping with no apparent thought for anything else. She must have some brains but she didn't appear to use them. He didn't think that reporting someone else would ever occur to her.

He eliminated Kitty and Gillie because they were French. He couldn't come up with any reason for them spying for France, but what did he know about international negotiations? But he thought there would be other people better placed to carry out that role. What, in any case, could anyone learn from a kitchen hand? He couldn't see how Kitty and Gillie would want to be informers unless they needed the money, but they were the best paid workers in the room, having been brought from Paris for their particular skills. They had probably been lured from France with money. Why else would anyone leave their family to come to a stink hole like Edinburgh? It didn't make them sound like very nice people, following money rather than staying with their loved ones, but who knew what their families had been like? They might have been glad to get away. And how can I criticise, thought Will, with my own background? He was beginning to feel like he had just been dumped in the kitchens when his mother had left with Lord Randolph. Dissatisfaction continued to smoulder within him. They hadn't considered taking him with them this time when they had every other time Lord Randolph had moved roles. What had been different this time?

Tom Croft and John Parlick were established Palace servants and, getting on in years, had more to lose than everyone else if they were turned out as informants. Will just didn't think they would do it.

That left Jennet and she was his friend. It was true that she was always asking questions but didn't lots of girls do that? She had a father somewhere locally but she didn't seem to visit him very often or he her. Most of the tine she slept like everyone else in the great hall and certainly never talked about anyone else. That didn't mean anything. Will never saw his own mother. Other than that, there was nothing against her. He forgot about the boys who tended the other fires in the kitchen. He didn't question himself either, though he realised there would be other people in the room who might do. He would be a suspicious character because of his knowledge about things a turnspit boy shouldn't really know. That had been a stupid mistake. Showing off again. Vanity.

No, sighed Will again. He never saw his mother. He was restless at night about that too. It was at night that he lay and wondered where she was. He had thought at first that she would be back when Randolph was forgiven his transgressions. The Queen seemed to pardon everybody else who plotted against her and in Randolph's case he was just passing on money from his own Queen. As a subject he could do no other. But neither of them had returned. Will had heard that there were other English gentlemen at the court. Were they Lord Randolph's replacements? He had heard the names ... Nicholas Throckmorton, Lord Drury. Could he ask them what had happened to Lord Randolph? Could he ask them to take him back to England? But, not only did he not know who these men were, he did not dare approach any of them. They were far above his station. He was just the turnspit and he knew his place.

EIGHTEEN

There was no sign of Bessie in the morning and no sign of Jennet either, but apparently someone had come in to say that Jennet was sick. So, she did have a family somewhere after all. She must have gone home to them the night before. Had she felt ill then? Will would have to ask her about it, when she got back.

`So, with both Jennet and Bessie missing, Tom Croft had to sort out who would do what that day. Minnie already chopped vegetables for Kitty's pies and so she took on the role of pottage maker. Kitty was kept on pie making for the morning but as Minnie was slow, one of the fire boys was brought in to help her for the afternoon. There wouldn't be many pies for those who enjoyed them, but pottage was what they had to produce the most of. At one point Will was sent to the bakery to ask for any stale bread they could give. Crumbled into the pottage, it would make the mixture stretch further, especially if they added extra water and a bit more salt. They did the best they could and felt pleased with themselves at the end of the day.

The conversation on every side throughout the day was largely about Bessie. Where was she? Where was she being kept? Would they let her go eventually? Was she being tortured?

At the end of the day, Kitty asked Will if he would help her take the waste to the midden. She knew she could carry the bucket quite easily herself and had always laughed inwardly at that soft girl Jennet. She had watched, amused, as Jennet had flashed her eyes so obviously at Will and Will had scarcely noticed the flirtation. Minnie could have helped Kitty but the notion of helping to carry the waste away hadn't ever crossed Minnie's mind, and it suited Kitty's purposes to manage without her. Kitty found Minnie a bit of a scatterbrain, though she was an amiable enough soul and would have been perfectly willing to help if asked. Kitty just didn't ask her.

Will was a bit of a dozy thing himself at times and just sat down as he usually did. He didn't even think about being with Kitty and not Jennet. Girls were not part of his thinking, though he did realise that they might be one day. Actually, when he did think of it, as soon as Kitty began talking, and as he had looked again at who was next to him on the trunk, he thought he liked Kitty much better than Jennet, though he didn't understand why.

And, he now worried that he wouldn't be able to impress Kitty with his knowledge of the world. He had forgotten that Kitty had worked at the French court in Paris and seen such people as Catherine de Medici and Diane de Poitiers and that maybe her experience was far superior to his. She was older than he was in the first place, not a lot, but enough for him to be impressed by her attention. No, Will had his own arrogance and worried, that he was on his own now. No Lord Randolph to quote.

'Will, I need to ask you a favour.' Will was hooked the moment Kitty said that. She needed him. That seemed important. He looked at her eagerly.

'Last night I went to Bessie's home in the town. I'd

said I would when I talked to her when she was taken away. I told her I would let her family know what had happened in case she wasn't released.'

'How did you know where she lived?'

'She told me when I first began to work here. I was new from France and I think she felt sorry for me on my own. She took me to meet her family. They were all very kind to me.'

Will was surprised. There were all sorts of things going on in that kitchen that he had no idea about. Nobody talked about personal things. Everyone was hugging something tightly to their chest. Derry was the same. And, he supposed, so was he!

'Well, she obviously wasn't released, was she, otherwise she'd have been back at work this morning?'

'I don't know, 'said Kitty. 'She might have needed to rest today after all the worry of yesterday. We don't know what happened to her. Her family didn't last night either when I went to see them. But she might have come home after I'd gone.'

'So, what can I do?' Will couldn't see why he was

needed.

'Well …' Kitty seemed to have lowered her voice and was leaning in towards him. 'I can't see why Bessie was taken, can you? There is something a bit strange going on, don't you think.'

Will said nothing. It seemed to encourage Kitty to continue.

'Last night when I went to Bessie's I felt as if I was being followed. I didn't see anyone when I set off and it was quite light then so that I felt safe enough. But when I was coming back, I got the same feeling again and this time it was dark. I was a bit scared.'

'What made you think there was someone there?'

'I don't know. It was just the impression I had. I've never felt like that before when I've been out in town. Not that I go out much anyway. But I promised Bessie's family that I would call in to see them tonight as well. To see if they had any news. To tell them if we had any.

'But we haven't. And Bessie's family probably

don't have any either.'

'Well, they might have heard where she is being kept. And in any case, I promised I would see them. I don't like to break a promise.'

Will was beginning to see how he was needed.

'So you want me to go with you?'

Kitty nodded and Will sat quietly as he thought. He was only slightly anxious. Nothing had happened to Kitty the night before and it would probably be fine again tonight. It might all be her imagination.

'I'll go with you,' he said finally. Kitty had been watching him closely, 'But I want something to eat before we set off.' He also thought it might be a good idea to 'borrow' a knife from the kitchen. He could replace it tomorrow. He could hide a small one up his sleeve like they did in the stories he'd heard when he was younger. The outing might even be exciting.

'Right, let's go now and have something quickly.'

As they walked off together, Will couldn't help looking around them. But it was already quite dark and the shadows of the Palace cast a murky obscurity over the midden yard. They neither of them heard the rustling of a nearby bush and they certainly didn't see the figure climbing out of it when the two of them had disappeared back into the Palace.

NINETEEN

It was Derry who had followed Kitty the night before and who had stepped out now from the obscurity of the bushes. It wasn't that he suspected Kitty of informing on Bessie or that she was up to something suspicious. It was more that he wanted to ensure that Kitty herself was safe. And that he was curious. His nose took him everywhere. He could have offered to accompany her wherever she was going, but that was not his way. He would not have known how to introduce himself. He hadn't seen anyone else loitering around the area and so assumed Kitty would be safe again tonight, but he decided to follow her and Will anyway, just in case. He hadn't intended to scare Kitty and he certainly hadn't wanted to push her towards Will. Derry wasn't jealous of Will, but he too liked watching Kitty's slender fingers and hearing the strange cadence of her French accent when she spoke Scots or English.

He knew they weren't going far. The worse thing would be the boredom of waiting for them while they made their visit. They were subdued for a while when they did finally emerge, which was a good thing as far as Derry was concerned as he wouldn't have been able to hear what they were saying. He was relieved when they decided to sit down again near the midden, though he couldn't get back to his original hiding place and had quickly to squat behind a tree. Good job that he was skinny. And that it was now dark. And he now had to slither further forward to be able to follow their conversation. Good job too that it hadn't rained for a while, otherwise he would have filthied his front or even rubbed holes into it, as it was exceedingly thin stuff.

'So, where is she then?'

Will seemed to have no answer.

'How can we find out?'

'If we knew who had taken her, we could maybe follow them. Would you recognise those two men again?'

'No, I don't think anyone from the kitchens would; otherwise they would have said. I suspect Bothwell is involved somehow, as it was him that Bessie kept shouting about. But I wouldn't recognise any of his men.'

Will wondered if he would even have been able to recognise Bothwell again. The man had ridden past so fleetingly on the day of the trial, his face hidden by the numbers of men who rode alongside. Bothwell had obviously been at his wedding, but Will had been working that day and had only had half his mind on observing. The only other time he had seen the man close to was through a keyhole when that document was being passed round to be signed. And that had been using just one eye. He couldn't be sure what the man looked like really close to. He was just a swarthy man with a neat moustache. There were so many like that.

'Did Bessie ever tell you where that other Bessie had been kept when Bothwell imprisoned her to have his way with her? It could be that our Bessie is being held in the same place.'

'Didn't Tom say that it was a barn?'

Kitty was jubilant. 'Yes, and didn't Gillie … I think it was Gillie … mention some names he'd heard talked about as Bothwell's men when he was at the Castle? I can't remember them though, can you?'

'No, but we could ask him.'

Suddenly, Kitty clapped her hands.

'How could I have forgotten? The best person to ask would be Toinette. She's maid to Lady Fleming who's now married to Lord Maitland. Do you know who she is? She's one of the Queen's own maids. She would surely know who Bothwell's men are. She must have seen them coming and going when Bothwell has been with the Queen.'

'You mean the Queen has a maid, who has a maid?'

Kitty laughed. 'Yes, why not?'

Will laughed with her. 'And does this friend of yours, Toinette, does she have a maid?'

'No, of course not. Stop teasing! Toinette was appointed in France like me. And came here, also like me, when her Majesty returned to Scotland. We were together on the boat coming across, leaning over the rail being sick side by side.'

'How lovely,' declared Will.

'We could go and see her. Well, you could come with me and then wait outside when I go in.' Kitty looked Will up and down and shook her head. 'I mean, you're not exactly presentable in your kitchen clothes, are you?'

Well, thank you,' he said, bowing. 'Good enough to protect you from danger, but not good enough to be acknowledged as your friend.'

Will was actually thinking of some of the clothes his mother had given him. They were in a chest somewhere in a storage room with his name and a padlock on the chest. He hadn't looked at them for ages. Would they still fit him? He had never thought to improve his appearance before.

'It's too late to go now. She'll be busy with the Queen's toilette or something. We could go tomorrow as soon as we have finished work.'

That would give Will time to find his chest and something more appropriate to wear. He rather fancied having a look around one of the posher rooms of the palace. A maid's maid would probably not have much luxury herself, but she might have access to more distinguished people's apartments.

Derry stepped out from behind the tree when Will and Kitty went off together. He had to stretch and arch his back to feel comfortable again. He had not really learnt anything for all his efforts, though he did feel that he might know some of the names of Bothwell's henchmen, if only his memory would work. He remembered Glennie coming into the kitchen one day and reporting that further placards were still being stuck up in the town. Names were being posted with claims that these men were Bothwell's associates in the murder of the Lord Darnley. But could he remember those names? Of course not. It was hard to remember names when you didn't know who any of them were. He wondered if Will and Kitty would know them? Or if they would recognise the names when Kitty's friend mentioned them? He would have to keep an eye on those two to see when they set off to visit the French girl. He wanted to follow them again. He waited a moment or two whilst they went to the great hall and then he too disappeared down the same ill-lit corridor.

TWENTY

Will managed to find both his chest in the store cupboard and something to wear which fitted him reasonably well. His elbows rubbed rather tightly against the cloth, the sleeves rode up from his wrists and his trews were somewhat shorter than was normal, but he felt he could pass in them. Derry hiding further down the corridor had to stifle his sniggers when Will reappeared and went to look for Kitty. Kitty didn't laugh. She knew very little about what passed for Scottish fashion and so nothing surprised her.

Toinette came to the door personally when Kitty knocked at where Lord Maitland and his wife resided in the palace. She looked shocked to see Kitty and had to ask who Will was. She seemed flustered and argued that she could not possibly allow them to enter. But Kitty argued and when Will could see that her friend was weakening, he joined in. Between them, they persuaded her to join them outside, though they had to give her time to finish her tasks and make her getaway.

She met them at the bottom of the corridor where Derry just had time to take himself off to somewhere out of the way. Will could think of no better place to take her than the tree trunk near the midden. It was at least a far enough distance from the Palace buildings and Derry happily could regain his old hiding place in the bushes.

Toinette's whole body was draped in a cloak which she even pulled around her face. Will was decidedly overdressed to sit near the midden and Kitty was much the same. They were as conspicuous as Toinette was not, though Toinette gave herself away by her agitated lack of composure. Will wanted to ask Kitty if the girl was normally like this.

Apparently not, as Kitty's first question was 'what's the matter? Why are you so restless?'

'Nothing,' said Toinette, fidgeting uncomfortably.

'Just tell me why you want to talk to me and then I can get back to my work.'

Will thought that telling the truth might set the girl

at ease. After all, what had she to fear? He couldn't see what was disturbing her.

'We simply would like you to help us with some names. We want to help one of our friends who has been taken away by some of the officers of the Palace and we would like to try and get her back.'

'She hasn't done anything wrong,' added Kitty urgently.

'I can't help you,' replied Toinette. 'I know nothing about anything.'

'We only need some names.' Kitty tried to reach for her friend's hand. She knew something was wrong. 'Come on, what's the matter? You're obviously worried about something.'

'I'm not.' It's just that I should be packing for my mistress. We are to hurry. We are leaving tomorrow.'

'Oh, that's fine. If you give us those names, we can be gone in no time. Where are you going to?'

'It's no business of yours. What names do you want?

Will had sat back leaving the conversation to Kitty and Toinette. But he didn't like this.

.'Now, just a minute' he said,' that's no way to talk. I thought you two were friends.'

'So did I,' said Kitty.

Toinette threw her arms around Kitty. 'I'm sorry. I'm so sorry. I didn't mean it. It's just that I think everything is going wrong and I'm frightened.'

'What's going wrong?' Will thought firmness was now needed. It was the strongest voice he could manage.

'I don't really know. Except that we are leaving tomorrow. My Lord Huntly asked the Queen for permission to leave today and was refused. So, My Lord Maitland is not asking for permission. He is just going. With my mistress and me. The Queen will be furious when she finds out. My mistress is in tears. You cannot leave the court without the Queen's permission.'

'And where are you going?'

'I'm not sure. I think Stirling.'

Will's response was an outburst. 'But that's where …' And then he silenced himself.

'Where what …?' That was Kitty and Toinette together.

'It doesn't matter,' said Will, 'If you can just give us the names of Bothwell's men.'

'I don't know any. I can't remember. I don't think they ever used their names with me.'

Kitty shook her head. I think that maybe she really can't remember. Not at the moment anyway. '

'Fine,' said Will. 'We'll just let her go back to her mistress, shall we?

Toinette was already leaping up from her seat and Kitty was going with her to the door back into the palace. Will watched them embracing and telling each other to keep safe.

'What was that all about?' asked Kitty when she returned and sat down again on the tree trunk. 'You know something that I don't.'

'I'm not sure. I think Stirling is where the Lords are all gathering to rebel against the Queen. I can't remember where I heard that or even who told me. But I think that's what's going on. They have already raised an army.'

Kitty quickly understood. 'So, if Maitland is leaving, even though he has no permission, it means he is abandoning the Queen and joining the Confederate rebels?'

'It looks like it.'

'Oh Lord. No wonder Lady Fleming is crying. She has been with the Queen nearly all her life. She first went to France when they were both children. They were playmates. She will be so upset about leaving her mistress. But she has to follow her husband. And Toinette will have to follow her.'

'And I know that Maitland has been with the Queen as long as she has been in Scotland. He was her mother's secretary before he became hers. Joining the rebel lords must have been a big decision for him. Things are getting very serious. The Queen will see him as a traitor. He could hang for it.'

'Another reason for Lady Fleming to be in tears.

But she will have to go with her husband. Will that make her a traitor as well?'

'I don't know. I really don't know.'

So, everything seemed to be coming to a head. Will personally thought that the Queen had been too soft. It was almost as if he had expected it, as if she deserved it, but of course, he couldn't say that. Mary supposedly spent a lot of her time crying these days. She had no energy, just stayed in her apartment rooms as much as she could. Was that Bothwell's fault or hers? Was she really ill? She had done nothing to punish the murderers of Rizzio when their identity was largely known to everyone at court. She even knew her husband had been involved. What sort of woman did that make her? She had ignored the proclamations on the placards in Edinburgh. She had just let them continue to feed the people with their foul accusations. Even John Knox had been able to denounce her from his church pulpit. It seemed he could say anything. It seemed that anyone could say anything. And then she had married a man, whom even Will thought was quite unsuitable for a Queen. And most people in town believed that that man, Bothwell, was her husband's murderer. Nobody had liked Darnley much, but strangely, now that his death was being ignored, he was becoming a cherished person amongst the populace. Things really couldn't look any worse. What a foolish woman the Queen had been! Will knew that she was largely hated now by all her people. And it wasn't just because she was a Catholic. She had been warmly welcomed back from France only five years ago and had turned everything she had touched since into as big a mess as possible.

But Will said nothing. He led Kitty back to the great hall for something to eat and tried to be cheerful. They may have achieved nothing, but they had learnt a lot. It seemed a civil war might be nearer than he'd thought. His stomach grew cold.

TWENTY-ONE

The Lord Bothwell had realised that too. People said the Lord Argyll had come in to tell him that the Confederate Lords were preparing to march on Edinburgh. They said the plan was to deliver the Queen from thraldom and bondage, to punish Bothwell as one of Darnley's murderers and to take over the baby prince for his own protection. It didn't seem to matter that many of the Lords ready to set out against the Queen had been involved themselves in the plot to murder her husband. These really were inexplicable times.

Bothwell must have immediately decided that Edinburgh Castle would be safer than remaining in Holyrood Palace and gave orders to his and the Queen's servants to prepare the move. But the shock for everyone next was that the Queen and Bothwell were refused entry into the Castle. It was for many an outrage, when they heard that. Who did this Balfour, the Governor of the Castle, think he was? The royal family had always used the Castle and

Holyrood Palace as their residences when in Edinburgh. News of the refusal whipped around the town and caused much jeering and even amusement, for many people knew that Bothwell had tried to get rid of Governor James Balfour of the Castle around the time of his marriage. He'd wanted to place one of his own men in the position, another Hepburn. But the Governor had refused to leave, not willing to be pushed around by the bully Bothwell. Bothwell had had to back down and leave Balfour in place, and now Balfour's resentment at the attempt to oust him had come back to hit Bothwell in the face. He got little sympathy. Balfour had obviously decided, like Maitland, to throw in his lot with the rebels. But many of the people were also aware that Balfour had been mixed up in Darnley's murder, though no-one quite knew how. He hadn't been in Edinburgh at the time of the crime. Now it was argued by some that access to the Castle for the rebels was part of a deal whereby Balfour could protect himself from the punishment which was coming Bothwell's way. So many of these rebels had backed Bothwell against Darnley and were now trying to save their skins. It was a cesspit of betrayal on every side. The Scottish lords were mired in so many different factions. Not one of them could be trusted according to the people Will spoke to. And according to Glennie too who brought them all this news, there was treachery on all sides and it all seemed to be going unpunished. The kingdom was lurching from one caastrophe to the next.

With no access to Edinburgh Castle, Bothwell obviously had to think again. The next news was that he had ordered that he and the Queen should be evacuated to Borthwick Castle, which was about twelve miles from Edinburgh, and apparently an excellent fortress where they could make ready their troops. Whispers from the Queen's party said he had commanded that some of her silver plate be melted down to raise money. Shockingly, the gold christening cup, which had been sent as a gift for Prince James's baptism from the English Queen, was also gone in the same way. Things really were becoming desperate.

Will wondered if he ought to be more worried. What would happen to all the Queen's staff if she lost any battles, was beaten to destruction? It was hard to imagine. What about those people who had been brought back from France when she had returned? People like Gillie and Kitty? What could he expect himself as an English man? The English had had nothing to do with this crisis but unsure crowds in a panic could behave in very unpredictable ways. Fear was beginning to seep slowly into Will's head, but Gillie and Kitty seemed oblivious. For a while, their work seemed to absorb them totally, until it became obvious even to them that things were changing.

Will's worries were answered in a way. The kitchen staff were stepped down. They weren't needed and no-one told them how long for. Food had to be provided for those people who remained behind, but apparently the Lord of Borthwick Castle had his own kitchens and could provide for his new guests. He was not asked for his opinion or even his permission. He probably had no desire to accommodate as many as now arrived but he had no choice. His royal guests began to empty his coffers, eating, drinking and preparing for battle at his expense. He would probably be ruined.

In the meantime, there was much more free time for those who remained behind at the palace. There was time to think. Kitty wanted to follow up their search for Bessie and got names off Gillie. Will happily agreed and they went off to look for Gillie's named people as soon as they had finished what cooking needed to be done for the day. Will was following Kitty out when there was a shout for him. To his astonishment, it was Derry. He stopped to let everyone pass out before him and hung back.

'What do you want?' He was brusque. Derry had chosen to ignore him for so long recently and that had rankled. He wasn't about to just let the boy walk back in from nothing again. Derry didn't seem to notice. He was at ease and smiling.

'I was hoping to come with you.'

'I don't think so.'

Kitty had turned back now and was watching them both, with questions all over her face.

'I know where you're going,' said Derry, 'I could help.'

'I don't think so,' repeated Will, annoyed, 'and in any case, we don't need your help.'

'It could get dangerous. I would be an extra person. You couldn't expect Kitty to help like that.'

Kitty bristled. 'I'm stronger than I look. Stop that. As for you, tell us what you think we're doing'.

'You're trying to find out where Bessie is being kept. You're going to visit the homes of those people who were named on the placards. I have a good idea about where would be the best pace to go to first.'

'How could you possible know that?' Will was indignant. Here was this lad boasting again. He had been right about most things when they had gone to

Kirk o'Field together. That had annoyed him then. It would be even more irritating if he was right now.

But he *was* right though, wasn't he? He knew exactly what he and Kitty had been planning. But how did Derry know and how could he claim to be able to tell them which was the best place to search?

'Well, I've been watching you again. Both of you. I followed you, Kitty, when you went to see Bessie. I just wanted to make sure you were safe in the dark'

'So, it was you,' Kitty exploded. 'But, you frightened me to death. I knew there was someone there.' She was ready to share Will's anger. Her fear from that night fueled her.

'It was me. I'm sorry. I didn't mean to scare you. Quite the opposite in fact.'

'And what else?' Will could not believe that Derry was so insensitive that he thought he could do anything he liked as long as he had his own good reasons. He seemed quite oblivious of any possible outcomes, any offence he might cause.

'I followed you when you both went to Bessie's

and then when you went to see that friend of yours, the French girl, who was crying. I was hiding just a bit further down the corridor.'

'I think you need tying up before we can go any-where in future'. Will's voice was hard. 'In fact, I could just do it now.'

'Wait!' exclaimed Kitty. 'Perhaps we ought to hear what he has to say about where we should go first.'

'He's just bluffing.'

Derry protested so much that Will dragged him as far away from the door as he could, away from any prying eyes and almost shook him against the wall.

'Right, tell us.'

It was a long and somewhat garbled tale. Derry was not at all unnerved, even with Will's rough han-dling. He said that he had heard Will and Kitty plan-ning to ask Glennie and Gillie for the names of those men condemned on the placards. So, he had got in first. Then he had asked around about where those men lived and even lengthened the list. He had thought into the night and drawn some conclusions.

'God's blood, you must have been busy.'

Derry nodded. 'But people had a lot to say. There's a lot of bad feeling about Bothwell out there.'

'We know. Tell us something we don't know. What did you find out?'

'Gillie remembered William Powrie, Pat Wilson and two men who might be brothers or father and son. I don't know ... Black Ormiston and Hob Ormiston. I got other names later. Someone called John Hay, another Hepburn ... no one could remember the right first name ... and a George Dalgleish. Oh, and that page Paris was involved in some of it too.''

'Do we know who these people are?' asked Kitty.

'Not really Except that they all seem to be in Bothwell's pay for whatever reason. Black Ormiston is his bailiff somewhere in East Lothian, but he works up here too. Don't know what he does. Powrie is a porter for him and we heard about Paris from Bessie. She told us he had had been badly treated by

Bothwell. Perhaps he had no choice but to help in the murder?'

'So, Mr Know-All, what do you suggest we do next?'

'Well, people directed me to a house in Blackfriars Wynd. It's where some of these men seem to have been lodging, but it was empty when I got there. A neighbour said that it hadn't been lived in for some time.'

'How do you always manage to find neighbours to tell you things?

'No idea. I'm just a kid. People just don't suspect me. Anyway, this neighbour told me that there is a farmhouse out beyond the town where they used to meet up. Actually, it isn't a farm, more a small holding, but didn't you say you were looking for a barn?'

Will looked at Derry sideways.

'You've been doing more than just watching and following us, haven't you? How do you know about the barn?'

'You said it was where Bessie was kept that time.'

246

Will nodded. That was true. Derry didn't seem to miss a thing. And he remembered everything too.

'So, what next? Do you know where this farm is?'

'I think so. If it's the right one. I followed some directions given to me and found a small place. But there were quite a lot of people milling around and I didn't want to go further as I would have been seen. It would be quite easy to get rid of me on my own. Nobody would miss me.'

'Quite right too,' thought Will, but Kitty was more sympathetic and hastened to reassure the rascal. Will scorned such sentimentality. Poor little Derry. Huh! He ought to be more friendly then.

'It looked like the men I saw were getting ready to move on. They were loading up their horses. They seemed excited. I didn't see Bothwell anywhere. Or Bessie.'

'Was there a barn?'

'There were huts and other outbuildings. You could easily keep someone in one of those.'

'Well. You can't have had much sleep. Are you

awake enough to take us to this place?'

But suddenly, out of the quietness of their whispered conversation, came a huge cheer from the main courtyard. Will understood instantly what it was. They had forgotten, and he wondered how they had missed the noise of the gathering. As they rounded the corner, they saw that the applause was for the arrival of the Queen and Bothwell. Horses had been made ready and were huffing and snorting eager to be on the move. Bothwell had already mounted and was guiding his horse to the front of the mass of riders and an equerry was helping the Queen into her saddle.

They were leaving for Borthwick and the Queen was going with them. Will noticed that she would be riding like a man. He was impressed. Pity she hadn't behaved more like a man in her government of the country. But straight away, he turned on his heels. Something had just sprung into his brain.

'We must get to that farm. That's why the men there were preparing their horses. They will be riding with Bothwell and the Queen to Borthwick. And if Bessie has been kept somewhere, what will they do with her now? She'll be no use to them anymore.'

'Oh, mon Dieu,' cried Kitty. 'If they leave her there, she will starve. Or they might even kill her.'

'Get moving!' Will gave Derry an almighty push. You'd better get us there as fast as possible.

TWENTY-TWO

It was agreed that they would leave Kitty at Bessie's house. They said they would collect her there later on the way back. Well, Kitty didn't actually agree, but they argued that she would be safer there and get in their way if they had to hide, crawl, who knew what would be necessary? She was still disputing the decision when they ran off and left her. She tried to run after them but became hampered in her skirts and, furious, was forced to stop. But she refused to give up and set off walking. Except she didn't know the way and when the path forked beyond the town, she sat down in a fury by the wayside.

When Will and Derry came to the farm it was in a clearing in a stretch of woodland. They bobbed down alongside an ancient fence and managed to hide amongst the long grasses. The view through the grasses was open and they were able to see many horses with men astride them, all milling about the yard and talking excitedly. It looked like the mount-ed horsemen were getting ready to leave but were waiting for something. There was a cart there too, loaded up with boxes, perhaps of provisions, perhaps of weapons. An older man sat ready to drive the mules which were to pull the cart. But then both Will and Derry gasped. This was what they had all been waiting for. A woman, nay a girl, they both recognised, was pulling someone out of what might be considered a barn, off to their right. They stifled that first gasp as soon as they could but another was ready to follow. With stretching and manoeuvring, they could just about see that the person who was being brought forth was another girl. It was a blind folded Bessie, being roughly manhandled and chiv-vied forward against her will into the back of the cart. She was pushed down and then covered with a large and heavy-looking black cloth. She was com-pletely hidden and looked like nothing more than a pile of old rags being kept dry under a tarpaulin. There was no movement, no struggling. The poor girl was probably labouring to breathe under the weight of it all. The first girl and the thug who had helped get Bessie into the cart then climbed up next to the elderly man at the front. That was the moment for them all to set off, the horses trotting along quite happily as if there was no rush, but fast enough for Will and Derry to have to work hard to keep up with them, hiding themselves well out of sight as they moved forward.

Kitty, sitting on a stump where the road had forked, heard the men and horses coming before she saw them. She had the common sense to hide herself behind a tree, not knowing who it might be. Will and Derry were far at the back so that she never saw them, but she had to catch her breath when she saw who was riding in the cart. She guessed that Will and Derry might have stayed behind to search for Bessie at the farm. Maybe they had even been caught? She didn't recognise anyone else, though for some reason felt suspicious of the covered bundle in the cart. Of course it could have just been vegetables or some other food stuff being kept safe from flies. But something, possibly boredom from sitting on the stump for so long, made her decide to keep pace with the cart and horsemen. If it led to nothing, she would go back to help Will and Derry later. It was hard at first to keep hidden on the open road but no-body seemed to be concerned with looking behind. They were all chattering and looking ahead to what-ever was to come. It was a lot easier keeping herself concealed when they reached the outskirts of the town. There were doorways to slip into and then more and more people to mingle amongst. There was a lot of hustle and bustle anyway, as the towns-people had to move out of the way of the horses.

Kitty couldn't decide where the group was taking her. They were even very near now to where Bessie lived so that her surprise was great when the cart turned off down an alley-way next to Bessie's tene-ment building, leaving the horsemen to continue along the main thoroughfare. She was even more startled when the cart came back again out of the alleyway only a few moments later and went off in the same direction as the horsemen. The covered lump in the wagon had gone.

Kitty was unsure what to do next. The alley-way was dark and uninviting. It was not the sort of place to venture down alone and the noises coming from it were muffled and disturbing as if there could be drunks or cut throats in the shadows, hiding out from the daylight. There was the familiar Edinburgh stink which made guessing what the way was used for easy. She had taken only a few tentative steps inside so that she could peer in a little further when there was shouting and her name was called. She turned and saw Will and Derry sprinting towards her. It took only a moment for her to tell them what she had seen and they were all three of them going forward into the blackness. The muffled noises had been Bessie struggling to get rid of her blindfold. They now saw that her hands had been tied behind her back too. The three of them identified themselves immediately as Bessie, in her panic and confusion, thought she was being set upon by those very same drunks and cut throats Kittie had feared and was making an almighty effort to fight them off. It seemed easier to bring Bessie out of the stinking foulness into the daylight than to try and explain to her in the dark.

Bessie, trembling and kicking, was finally manoeuvred into the daylight and scarcely seemed to recognise her three liberators. When she did, she just cried and trembled even more. Kitty hugged her and she eventually allowed herself to be led to her home. She walked in stunned silence. Only her sister was there with her baby, Bessie's niece, and she was overcome with emotion. That made the two sisters useless in dealing with the family crisis. Bessie seemed to be thirsty more than anything else. She didn't want to eat and was certainly not able to talk. Kitty could only look her all over and pronounce that there were no obvious injuries, beyond the friction rope burns around her wrists. She didn't appear to have been tortured. There was nothing much she could have told her gaolers, but they hadn't known that and might have tried anyway. It was still a mystery as to why they had taken her in the first place. They would have to wait for Bessie's later account of what had happened.

Will thought that they had now found out who the kitchen informer had been, but not one of them said a word as they trudged back to the Palace. They knew who the sneak was, but they didn't know why she had been there amongst them. And Will still didn't feel comfortable with Derry and was reluctant to discuss the events of the day with him.

All three were gloomy as they walked back to the Palace. The court yard was almost empty. Only piles of drying dung now showed that such numbers of horses had ever been there, and an undergardener was shovelling that up into a wheelbarrow as they passed through. The palace corridors were quiet too and even the kitchens, which usually bustled with warmth and commotion, seemed subdued. People with families in the area had drifted off to see them and only Gillie, Tom Croft and one of the fire boys remained. Tom was reviewing the store rooms and trying to work out how to preserve the things they already had which might not now be needed and how to contact their providers to stop the arrival of more. His problem was that nobody knew how long this state of affairs might continue.

Derry had gone off as soon as they arrived back in Holyrood, with no mention of where he was going. Fair enough, thought Will, back to how things usually were with the lad. He wondered what Derry could be investigating now. At least he wouldn't be spying on them in the meantime. In the kitchen, Kitty informed Tom that it was unlikely that Jennet would be coming back.

'How do you know?'

'We saw her going off with a crowd of men on horseback. We're guessing that she was going to join Bothwell's party. Perhaps she was going to Borthwick?'

'Goodness!' exclaimed Tom. He was silent for a moment as if he was thinking exactly what Will and Kitty had thought earlier. But he didn't say anything about his conclusions. Neither did Will and Kitty. Who knew what the mood of the people in the Palace and in the town was now? Yesterday, nearly everyone seemed to have turned against their Queen, but now that she had been challenged and was perhaps in danger, they might have been moved to support her again. The mood of the people could turn on the throwing of a coin. That was one of Will's memorable remnants from Lord Randolph. It was safer to show no allegiance.

Kitty said that she thought Bessie would be back as soon as she was well and cut the story short. Tom was just pleased that she was safe and no more curious than that. He seemed to understand that there were things going on that he really didn't want to know. Kitty said that she would go and visit Bessie sometime to see if she could find out when she might be returning. It had occurred to her that Bessie might refuse to return if she thought she might have to work alongside her abductor again. Will had no idea what to do with himself and asked if he could help in any way in the kitchens. He ended up going with Tom to choose some meats to roast for those people who were still in the palace. There were more than he'd realised … most of the servants, the wives of those lords who lived at Holyrood and had ridden off that morning, quite a few children, and people like the chamberlains and pages who did not usually eat in the great hall There were lots of hangers-on whom Will had never heard mention of before. The Palace was like an aimless and crowded city.

The atmosphere in the great hall was sombre, everyone absorbed in their own thoughts. There was anxiety about the future and no news about what was going on beyond Edinburgh.

The kitchen staff reported for work each morning and did what was required of them. They had never had so little work and began to worry about whether they would ever be paid. Glennie came flouncing in as usual even though they already had an abundance of wood. It was as if he were trying to maintain that nothing had changed in the world. But it was Glennie in the end who brought the first bit of news. It might just have been rumour for all they knew, but it was all they had and they fed upon it with relish, even though it did not bode well.

Apparently, the Lords had massed in front of Borthwick Castle and discharged several volleys of musketry. That sounded as if it had just been merely for effect. The soldiers had called for Bothwell to show himself and take up a man to man challenge. The servants weren't sure quite what that meant but in any case, Bothwell never appeared, whereupon the soldiers began shouting out that he was a traitor, a butcher and a murderer. The story was that Bothwell had looked out earlier and grasped at once that he was easily outnumbered. Estimates were that there were over seven to eight hundred men gathered before the castle, all fully armed and eager for blood, his blood. It must have been obvious to him that if he were captured when the castle was taken, he would most surely be killed.

People now scorned Bothwell's next action when it

was relayed to them. Bothwell had apparently turned tail and crept out through some gate at the back of Borthwick Castle. He galloped away under the very noses of the assailants. That might have been amusing if you had been on Bothwell's side but he was now roundly abused for leaving his Queen to fend for herself. The insurgents now called to the Queen to abandon her husband and accompany them back to Edinburgh. They would help her to find and punish her former husband's murderers. Mary went up onto the castle walls and proudly refused.

Mary had refused. What on earth did that mean? Did she really care for Bothwell? If she did care, then most people despised her for it. The soldiers certainly did and apparently began to shout all kinds of degrading insults to her. But they would not attack her. That remnant of royalty that she still held must somehow have restrained them. She may have been a dissolute woman in their eyes, but she was still a queen. The gathered men turned around and took themselves back to Edinburgh. They were not interested in attacking the Queen on her own. Glennie said they would be arriving soon. He somehow knew where Borthwick was and how long it would take the army to return. Tom Croft got himself into a flurry then, wondering if he ought to start preparing food for them.

Whilst Tom went off to see if he could find out what was going on, the other kitchen workers heard Glennie tell the rest of the tale. When the soldiers had gone, the Queen must have made her escape. She had apparently disguised herself as a man and in the black of night had slipped out of the castle and made her way to somewhere nearby called Cakemuir, where she had met up with Bothwell again. There were tales of her descending the castle walls in a basket but that seemed too far-fetched. The two of them had then made their way together to Dunbar.

What a story! The staff didn't know whether to cheer or lament. Later, Kitty remembered that Mary had always liked dressing up and that in her younger days she had several times joined other disguised friends to trip around Edinburgh incognito. Her costume had often been as a man. She delighted in deceiving people into thinking she was other than she appeared. There was always something to surprise him, thought Will, about this strange and enterprising queen, who had not long before been prostrate on her bed in her distress and who was now probably laughing into the wind at her clever getaway.

According to Tom, the Confederate Lords as everyone was now calling them were going to stay briefly at the Castle whilst they considered their next move, so that there was still little for the staff at Holyrood to do. There was no challenge from Balfour at the castle. He had obviously decided to side with the Confederates. Nobody questioned the turn around. Was everyone mad Will asked himself?

Crowds turned out to greet and cheer the Lords. Will and Kitty, with more free time to do as they wished, were amongst them and Derry, Will guessed, would be there somewhere too, sneaking into corners and along the back streets, doing his usual eavesdropping and snooping. The main gathering was at the Mercat Cross where several of the Lords declared that the sole reason for their having taken up arms was to enable the murderers of the late King to be pursued. They then produced a proclamation urging that all citizens should join them in their noble challenge to the oppression of the Lord Bothwell.

TWENTY-THREE

Eventually, an uneasy calm fell upon the city but it was not for long. Kitty and Will had gone to sleep in the great hall. They had both been overtaken by the exhaustion of a long and satisfying day. They had done what they had set out to do, freed Bessie and returned her to her family. Will was breathing heavily in a dead to everything sprawl when he was bumped awake by Derry. He growled seeing Derry, his finger on his lips, motioning for him to follow him outside into the corridor. Waking up to Derry was bad enough. This inconstant friend was not what he wanted to see at this God forsaken hour.

'What now?' he said, showing his bad temper.

Derry, indifferent to the fact that he had been missing all day and with no explanation for his absence, told him that the army was leaving. Now, at that very moment.

'So? I'm not a soldier. What's it to me?'

'Well, I just thought we might follow them.'

'You mean *you* want to follow them and want me

to keep you company? Two's safer than one?'

Derry, of course, was unable or unwilling to answer and just tugged at Will's chemise. 'Come on or we'll miss them.'

'What if we do?'

'But think of the excitement.'

'I can do without it, I'm sure.'

'Come on. You'll regret it if you don't'

'Regret getting up when I've only just gone to sleep?'

Derry was still tugging at him even as he was searching for something to wear. Somehow, he had made the decision to go with Derry but his body was still wondering why.

In the corridor, still trying to comprehend what he was doing, he began breathing properly again, takI'ng stock of what the two of them were about to do.

'We can't just disappear,' he said, we need to let someone know where we are going.'

'Who?'

'Perhaps Tom. Or Kitty, who can then tell Tom'

'Kitty will just want to come with us. Remember what happened last time.'

'Right. Well you find Tom and I'll get my things together.'

'So, you're coming?'

'Looks like it,' said Will, hardly believing it. He found his way to the kitchen, where one of the fire boys was fast asleep alongside the turnspit fire. It was the boy's job to keep the fire going all night but it looked as if he'd fallen asleep in the warmth. Will threw another log on the embers, which should keep the fire going until the real morning and save the boy from a thrashing. He reached over the sleeper to tinker with the bricks near his stool to get some of his saved money. He hoped he'd be back because he left the major part of his stash behind and felt uneasy about it. He was beginning to realise that following soldiers was not a wise thing to do. Soldiers invariably thought with their fists or their weapons and rarely with their brains.

'Where are your things?' he asked Derry when they met up again.

'I haven't got anything worth bringing.' The lad was overdressed for the time of year but then so was Will. It was the only method they had of taking extra clothes with them but neither could admit the penury of it. Will had filched that short knife again from the kitchen. He wondered if Derry had any kind of weapon up his sleeves.

They were just in time to tag themselves on to the end of the soldiers' line. There were other people clustered there too, who were obviously not part of the army. Perhaps they had also answered the call to the populace from the Lords for those civilians who could, to aid them in hunting down Bothwell? They carried all sorts of weapons … pitchforks, spades, broom handles. They looked a sorry lot. On the other hand, Will and Derry didn't visibly carry anything at all either. There were women too, including one heavily pregnant, red faced, and tired from the out-set. Perhaps they were women who had no life away from their menfolk? Perhaps they were there to scavenge after the battle? Will had heard that stealing from corpses filled lots of poor people's pockets. He wouldn't have been surprised if that had been Derry's reason for being there.

After marching for some time, they noticed that the pregnant woman had been taken up onto one of the carts. They were impressed by that and, thereafter, walked alongside all the carts asking repeatedly for lifts. They were refused every time, and not always very politely. They became indignant, mostly because they couldn't see any good reason for the rejections and in the end, when one of the carts was rounding a corner and the carter needed to concentrate on a little steering, they heaved themselves up onto the back and sat there, legs dangling free. It was an excellent observation post from which to see that what they had perceived as marching was in fact nothing of the sort. It was in reality a raggle-taggle jumble of human beings walking in scrambled rows and at varied pace and stretching out haphazardly as far as they could see. It was hardly a disciplined army. The people Will and Derry had joined seemed as ragged and bereft as they were themselves. There was little conversation, all of them tired, worn and beginning to wonder why they had come. It wasn't their argument. Life would go on as drearily as it always had whoever was in charge. Will and Derry were also beginning to question their own presence. Well, Will certainly was. Why had he ever agreed to follow Derry? There was nothing in it for him. Even if he survived the expected battle, a tough challenge with just a puny knife down his sleeve, what would come next? There would be no job to go back to; he would be isolated forever from his mother; would he be expected to enrol for good in this nonsensical army? And he would be stuck with this mad Derry, whose friendship warmed hot and cold and was on nobody's side but his own. He had been an idiot. He blamed his semi-asleep state when Derry had tugged at him.

He began to look around to see if there might be an

opportunity to slip away. After all, they were at the back of the convoy. A quick jump and he could be lying low in the heather. But, how would he get back to Edinburgh? The walking wasn't the problem. The problem was that he had led too sheltered a life and was lost now in a childish panic as soon as he ran into a first trouble. The road to his present difficulty had not been a straight one. That was his issue. But as he considered his surroundings, he discovered another. He realised that the barrels bouncing alongside them on the cart did not contain food stuffs, or even weapons. He nudged Derry. Neither of them could read but they could recognise gunpowder barrels when they saw them.

That was when it came home to them that this was not just some little jaunt into the countryside. They were riding along to war, a war which might swallow them whole and leave them either dead or adrift of everything they'd ever known. And what did they do? Nothing. They just sat there, dazed and in silence, leaving, it seemed, fate to look after them.

Well, at least until they got to wherever they were going and then they might think again.

The long caravan eventually straggled to a stop. Most people wandered over to the heather where they relieved themselves, even the women, regardless of who was watching. The heather steamed its pungent fumes in the hot sun. It was scorching, the sun directly overhead. Derry and Will watched with envy as most people around them drank from little pots and rested further away from the road, wise at least to avoiding the urine sodden plants. Some were even eating. Will and Derry had nothing. They had neither of them thought to bring any kind of food or drink, so used as they were, to food being provided at need in the great hall. There must have been someone there who had been equally negligent in providing for himself but who was evidently more adept at looking after himself, for that someone shouted that he had found a stream and Will and Derry stumbled forwards, followed by a number of others who must have been equally thirsty. Some sauntered over to refill their pots. They drank with their mouths in the water, sniffing at the brackish taste, appreciating the cold and wetness of it. They saw, as they raised themselves up, that the stream was running some distance away into a much wider river. Someone announced that it was the River Esk.

Why had they come to a stop? Was it for the rest they all needed? Will walked ahead and round the side of another hill and saw laid out before him that the confederate army had gathered up behind lots of banners and, horrifyingly, he caught his first sight of the enemy, the royal army lined up on the hill opposite. He didn't feel it as the enemy though. After all, it was the Queen, who supposedly paid his wages. Why had he come to fight the woman who fed him?

It looked as if somewhere between the armies was where they were going to fight. Under a blazing sun, off two hillsides and on his side at least, with an army that consisted of a large number of untrained soldiers, if they could even be called soldiers, when they were hot, tired, unarmed and unsure of their allegiance.

Will went further forward to look at a huge banner held aloft at the front. It showed a young child in prayer beside a mutilated corpse, all on a white background. The child was praying with words coming out of his mouth but Will's inability to read meant that the words were meaningless to him, and to many of the others waiting with him, he guessed. Pointing forward, he asked a man sitting astride his horse what the prayer was. Anyone riding a horse must have had some education, more than he had, at any rate.

'Judge and avenge my cause, O Lord', he was told, the man adding, 'it's what we fight for. Our wee Prince James wanting us to avenge his father's murder.'

Will thanked the gentleman. He dared to ask 'what is this place?'

'Carberry Hill, young lad'.

It meant nothing to him. He looked more seriously at the banner. So, the corpse was supposedly that of

King Darnley and the child was the son he had with Mary. What a nonsense! The real child was no more than a baby, neither able to kneel or pray as shown. So, the words of the prayer were a concoction. All was false, made only to inflame people. The soldiers beyond, waiting at the very front were more seriously armed and Will could see their pikes standing upright ahead. Similar pikes rose upwards at the front of the enemy lines. He shuddered as a picture of the fighting formed in his imagination. He saw the poor people at the back of the line fighting these awesome weapons. They would be struck dead before they even got near the men who were supposed to be their enemy opponents. He could almost feel the pointed end of a pike piercing his stomach, the blood trickling down his poorly clothed body. And then he asked himself why these poor fellows should care about Darnley's death, murdered or not. Darnley would never have cared about them. Even he didn't care about Darnley.

As he walked back to find Derry, Will noticed the

smaller banners of the army across on the hill, the blue cross of Scotland, the cross of Saint Andrew and there was a banner with a red lion standing up-right, which he was told by someone, marked where Queen Mary would be. He thought of the Queen now. Was she in armour too? Her sun struck hair would be shining gloriously against the fierce metal. He wondered again why he had followed Derry so readily. He really must have been half asleep for he now saw that it was all madness.

He found Derry sitting amongst some of the town people they had walked with. He had pushed himself out of the sun under the cart they had travelled on but the discomfort of it showed on his face. And the gunpowder barrels were still there above him. Being crushed alongside others under there could scarcely be any cooler. He had obviously forgotten about the barrels of gunpowder. Could the heat of the sun work on them?

Nothing seemed to be happening and the afternoon wore on. The expectant atmosphere of only hours before was draining away into a desultory lack of interest in anything. It was too hot.

People began to pass by walking back in the direction they had come from. Will wondered what was happening. In the end, he asked where they were going.

'Home', one said.

'I can't see anyone fighting today' said another.

'All they're doing is parleying.'

'And it's getting us nowhere.'

'I want to get home before it's dark.'

'Where's home?' shouted Will, as they slowly moved away from him.

The answer came back faint now, but he heard it 'Edinburgh'. It was all he needed. He ran back to find Derry.

'Come on' he shouted, we're off back to Edinburgh.'

But Derry was shaking his head. Will looked at him, his face questioning his friend's reasoning. They had no food, no water, except what amounted to a bog, and Derry wanted to stay. Why? If the lad ever returned safely, Will would ask him but he, Will, was going. He'd made his decision. To the devil with Derry. The lad could sort himself out. Let him explode under those great gunpowder barrels.

TWENTY-FOUR

Those walking back were downcast. Will couldn't understand it. He felt happier than he had felt all day. He was going to live. He had left his anxiety behind. Will fell into step with a young man walking alone. Neither said anything for a while. The man marked his path with a broom handle which must have been his intended weapon. It served him better now as a staff over the rough ground.

'You wouldn't have got far with that,' Will finally observed.

'I know,' the man replied and cast a look at Will. 'But what have you got?'

'Just a knife down my trews.'

The man looked back at him scornfully. 'So we're both better off going home'

'I don't know why I came,' said Will. 'It's none of it my argument.'

'Me neither. You just get caught up in the excitement and come to your senses lying in your own muck on the battlefield. If you come to your senses

279

at all. And the leaders you've followed are gone, left when they saw the way things were going.'

'I agree. You have your head fixed on right.'

The man smiled. 'Well, at least I turned up and was counted. 'I've served my dues. Who do you serve?'

'No-one,' answered Will, wondering what the man meant.

'Then, you have no cause to be here. Do you not have a clan chief'?'

Will shrugged. He really had no idea what the man was talking about.

'No-one to answer to? No-one you have to pay your rent to?

Will shook his head.

'Well, you're lucky then. I'm supposed to fight for my landlord. He gets my rent money and my death if I die on the battlefield. I don't know what I get from him. His protection they say, but I don't feel that. Nor do my bairns. My neighbours have seen that I turned up. Let's hope that they will declare for me if I'm missed. That will have to do.'

The man said no more and Will trudged alongside him for a while. The jubilant enthusiasm of the march off to battles had long subsided and even though Will knew he was now safe, the despondent atmosphere many others seemed to feel reached him and seeped into his brain. He began to worry about Derry. Did Derry even have any kind of weapon if he had to fight? He should have leant him the knife. Guilt began to gnaw at him. He had abandoned the only friend he had. Was Derry a friend?

Further on, he began to notice men joining their group higher up and coming in from across the heather. They all now walked in common together and in dull conversation. Will nodded a sort of goodbye to his companion and walked faster ahead until he reached the newcomers and could follow their talk. He could see many more coming from the same direction.

'They're doing nothing but parley. It doesn't seem to be getting anywhere.'

'They're trying to organise challenges to personal

combat, but that's not working either.'

'My Lord Bothwell did say he would fight anyone who came forward from the enemy, but nobody came.'

'I heard different. I heard somebody came; I don't know who, but her Majesty would not accept the challenge. I heard said that the challenger was not worthy enough to fight him.'

'Well, that's when I left. They're all a set o'ditherers on both sides.'

So, all these men, Will realised, who were now happily chattering together were meant to be enemies. The newcomers were from the Queen's party and were melting away from their army just as Will was slipping away from his. The Queen's supporters had no more heart to fight than Will's side. And from the talking he heard around him, there was little enmity between them either.

As the walkers reached the outskirts of Edinburgh, individuals nodded to their companions and disappeared off to outlying homesteads and then down lanes and streets until Will himself veered off on his own solitary route as they neared Holyrood Palace. He felt empty and stupid, the man who had marched off to war and come back as dispirited as if he had personally lost the battle. So different from how he had set out.

He followed his own footsteps, not knowing what to do. It now occurred to him that he might not even have a job to go back to. He had trusted Derry to inform Tom Croft that they were answering the call to arms, but what if he hadn't? Derry had never proved his reliability to him. He realised now that they had left Tom in the lurch. There would have been no Jennet and no Bessie when they'd gone. Tom would have been low on staff and justifiably annoyed.

The corridors of the Palace were dark and gloomy as Will approached the kitchens. His own kitchen was warm and busy before him as he stepped inside. He could see everyone involved in their jobs. He smiled over at Kitty and Minnie. Gillie, as always, was absorbed in whatever sauce he was making. He saw that Bessie was back. She seemed different somehow. She merely raised her eyes, nodded a sort of smile and then resumed her chopping. There was no Jennet. And where he and Derry should have been, he saw the two fire boys. The sight struck him into silence. He just stood there on the threshold. He had evidently lost his job, and for what?

He might have turned round and left if the smiles of Kitty and Minnie hadn't awoken Tom Croft to Will's presence.

'Ah,' said Tom, you've come to your senses. I don't understand you. Why follow an army when no one obliges you to? There's no honour in that.'

'At least, he's shown some sense,' said John Parlick. 'That Derry is still missing. And you've made it back before the army has even got here. How did you manage that? We've been told to prepare a meal for them for late tonight.'

John was looking at Will as he spoke, but Will had no answer to give. How did anyone in the kitchen know that the army would be coming back that day?

'Derry wanted to stay with the army,' Will answered. 'I don't know why? Did he tell you we were going?'

Tom nodded. That was at least something.

'That Derry has a nose that's too long for him,' John went on.' I've bumped into him all over this place. He's everywhere he has no reason to be and he never has an answer when I've asked him why?'

'Well, you're lucky this time,' said Tom. 'I'm going to leave Billy and Jamie where they are and you can take Jennet's place. It doesn't look like she's coming back. It's a good job I know you're a good worker.' He grinned as he paused and added, 'most of the time.'

They could probably all see the relief on Will's face. They all knew that he had no home to go to if he were thrown out of the Palace. And as he got himself organised to work in Jennet's place, Will realised that Jennet's job merited more pay than his as a spit turner. Perhaps he wouldn't get the extra money though, because of his absence. He didn't dare ask, though he did notice that the two fire boys had now been elevated to being addressed by name.

TWENTY-FIVE

The day over, Will was eager to get to the great hall for something to eat. He was ravenous, but hadn't dare filch anything in the kitchen. He was on his best behaviour and felt Tom's eyes constantly upon him. Very little had been said as they worked. There was a tension running through them all as if the harmony they had hitherto enjoyed together had cracked and needed time to repair. Will understood by what talk there was that there had been no battle at Carberry Hill and that both armies were returning to Edinburgh, but nobody knew how that had come about or what the outcomes had been for both sides. This ignorance added to the tension as everybody waited for the soldiers to arrive back to find out what had actually happened.

Bessie was the first out of the door when their work was done. There was none of her usual banter, her teasing, her loud, usually benign, criticisms of whoever had annoyed her that day.

Tom shook his head sadly. 'She's not the same

person since she came back.'

Will would have been gone himself next if Kitty hadn't called his name. He held back and she joined him and sat down near the door. He felt obliged to sit too.

'I'm glad you're back safely,' Kitty began, 'and so pleased there wasn't a battle. That should mean Derry is safe too.'

'What's the matter with Bessie?' Will asked. 'She seems altered.'

'Perhaps she just needs time? That was a dreadful ordeal for her in that barn.'

'Has she said what happened to her?'

'Not really. I went round to see her last evening but she didn't say much. She was kept in the barn all the time and asked lots of questions. I think they sus-pected her of being part of a conspiracy against Bothwell.'

'Part of a conspiracy? Bessie? She wouldn't have been able to keep a secret in her head for any longer than it took her to say it out loud to whoever was with her.'

'Well, I think she's learnt that lesson. She doesn't say much anymore. Perhaps she'll slowly come out of it. I don't think anyone hit her or touched her in any way… you know what I mean … not like her cousin. She was fed well enough. It was Jennet who brought her food to her.'

'Ah, yes, Jennet. We saw her at that farm, didn't we? How did she come to be there? Did Bessie know?'

'I saw Jennet too. She was driving the cart when they brought Bessie back home. She was obviously part of whatever was going on. She apparently treated Bessie quite well.'

'But why did they take her in the first place? And how did Jennet get to be involved'

'Bessie thought that she was related to one of the men there. Maybe to more than one of them. They all seemed to be Bothwell's liegemen. Perhaps Jennet told them that Bessie was always criticising Bothwell?'

'Well, she wasn't the only one was she? And Jennet kept that quiet didn't she? We all thought she had no relations locally. Maybe we'll get to know more later when Bessie is back to herself. I doubt Jennet will be returning though. She wouldn't dare. She certainly can't hope to get her job back. I've been lucky there.'

'Yes, and I wonder what will happen to Derry? He should be back by now if he returned with the soldiers.'

They looked for Derry in the great hall but there was no sign of him, although there were plenty of returning soldiers milling everywhere. He did not appear throughout the next day either and Tom, short of staff and needing to fill the fire boys' places, had gone out and found two new workers in Edinburgh. He brought back two unkempt and dirty tenement urchins and sent Will off to the water pumps with them to oversee their washing. They neither of them liked the water on their faces but Will found the strength to control their wriggling and made

290

them remove all their rags and even washed their hair with some coarse soap Kitty had found for him.

They were lucky it was the summer. The same job in winter would have been a much greater hardship, for Will as well, as the boys flayed into him and Will's own clothes were soaked through. Finally, Will realised that the boys could not wear their old rags and so he made them hide naked in the bushes whilst he went to his own clothes chest and selected some clothes he didn't think would fit him any longer. The boys, transformed, were then fed, and they ate as if they had never seen food before. The skinniness of them suggested that they probably hadn't seen much that was worth eating in their past lives.

They would begin to learn their jobs the next day. For now, they were shown into the great hall and given a pallet to sleep on. Will told them to stay there until the morning, but he did wonder if they would be waiting for him when he came back for them then. Their temptation might be to creep off during the darkness. But they were there when Will came looking for them. They must have realised that they were better off in the palace than outside struggling for their survival. They were eager, but still nameless. They, in their turn, had become 'the boys.'

Derry turned up in the kitchen later that day and stood on the threshold for a moment looking round. He must have seen that there was a full complement of workers but he remained standing there a while longer. He seemed to be wondering what to do. Everyone paused in what they were doing and looked back at him, just as uncomfortable in the moment as he was. Then, without a word, Derry turned and was on his way out when Tom called out.

'Derry, I'll see you later in the great hall. Wait for me there.'

Derry didn't stop. There was the slightest nod of his head seemingly acknowledging that he had heard but he kept on going and conversation returned to the room. Only Tom stood fixed in thought. He was thinking about how he had found Derry. He was the only person, apart from Derry himself of course, who remembered that day. Derry had never spoken of it, as he never spoke of anything much in his life. Even Tom didn't know where Derry had come from before he began working in the kitchen.

Tom had found Derry like he had found 'the boys', like he had found many of his lowly workers. He went looking among the poor families. There were so many of them. Most parents were glad to hand their boys over to him. It was almost a relief for them to have a child taken off their hands, one less mouth to feed, one less child to clothe. They asked few questions. It didn't mean that such families didn't care about their offspring as many thoughtless people tried to argue. They knew their children would likely fare better taken in by the Palace. Tom told them their lads would be fed and clothed and would sleep at the Palace. They would receive little as a wage but it was at least a reliable amount of money and it was a burden less for the families they came from.

Derry hadn't been like that. There was no family when Tom had asked to see them for their permission to take their son. He knew Derry had been on his own, a scavenger of middens and other rubbish dumps. That was where he had found the boy one day, searching through the midden in one of the palace yards. Derry had thought he was in trouble at first, caught for stealing off Palace 'property'. He was caught red handed clinging to a discoloured cooking pot coated with green, slimy offal. Tom had taken him by the ear, washed him and hauled him in for something to eat. There were lots of hard and cruel men in Edinburgh, but Tom wasn't one of them. Derry hadn't even had any personal things to collect from wherever he slept at night before going off with Tom. He had sold every little keepsake which he might have had from his mother or sister. Tom had found a job for Derry at the time and, as he thought about the lad, he wanted to find one for him now. Otherwise he might be reduced to scavenging the middens again.

Tom knew that it had to be a proper job. The Palace would not pay for meaningless activities, however pitiful the amount. He decided now that Derry could be the kitchen's official water carrier. The 'boys' currently brought in water, alongside keeping the fires fed, but there was never enough. Tom argued now that shortages slowed the work of the kitchen down, as the cooks waited for water to boil their vegetables or thin the pottage. Sometimes, it was even used for washing hands, though hygiene wasn't much of an issue in the kitchen. It was enough that everyone's hands looked clean. Water carrying wasn't a pleasant job, especially in the winter, when the pump sometimes froze and had to be coaxed into life again. Ice cold water would slop over the sides of the buckets, no matter how careful you tried to be. And water was heavy too so that your arms ached. Derry's arms would surely ache as he was a such a skinny thing, but the job was the best Tom could think of and Derry would have to get used to it. He would have to if he wanted to stay within the Palace. And Derry did. Tom had gone to see him as soon as he could and was just leaving as Will and Kitty arrived in the great hall in search of their friend. Before he took his leave, he pulled Will to one side.

'I'm glad I've seen you. I forgot to mention it when we were working. Someone arrived with a message for you whilst you were away. You were askcd to go and see somebody but there was no name given. I said I would give you the message on your return but they said no matter; they would come again to collect you another time. They haven't come back yet.'

Will was intrigued. He couldn't think of anyone who knew him beyond the kitchens. 'So you don't know who it was?'

Tom shook his head. 'I didn't recognise him from anywhere. In any case, it was someone's page or valet or manservant. You were being asked to meet with another person, not him. He was possibly English. He spoke rather like you.'

Will knew that this was important, whether for good or bad, but Tom was already moving away. Besides, the hall was noisy with excited soldiers and their friends eager to welcome them back and hear the battle news. He somehow knew that he would be worrying until the messenger returned for him. But what could he do now? Kitty and Derry were there in front of him and he was just as eager as the other hall people to hear what Derry had to say. He didn't want to miss any of Derry's account of where he'd been all this time. The soldiers had been back long before him. What had he been up to in the mean-time?

'I came back with the soldiers,' Derry began. 'There was no battle.'

'Yes, we've heard that, but why not?

'Well, after you'd gone, I crept right up to the front of our side and tried to listen to what was going on. Men were slipping away all the time. You saw them too.'

I was one of them'.

'Yes, well it seems the same thing was happening on the other side.'

'It was. Men from their side came and joined us as we returned. We all walked back together. We all got on well too, which shows that we are not really enemies. It's the lords who do all the arguing, not people like us. What would any of us gain from a battle like that?'

'Anyway, with all the men leaving, it meant that there weren't enough fighters to give a victory for either side. That's why they decided not to fight. So, the decision was made that we would go back to Edinburgh.'

'Together?'

'Yes. The Queen was brought across to our side with some of her people. People were saying she'd surrendered.'

'Oh, my poor lady.' This was Kitty, but the two lads were not so sympathetic.

'She didn't look so poor when she arrived. She came with her high and mighty airs and we could hear her cursing the lords around her.'

'And where was Bothwell all this time?'

'Oh, he had ridden off before the Queen came over to us. Some of the men said he and the Queen had embraced in front of them. She had refused to give him up.'

Kitty snuffled again. They both ignored her. Derry continued.

'It began with everyone, the lords, I mean, treating the Queen with her due respect, but then the ordinary rebel soldiers began cursing her. They were shouting all sorts of foul things, calling her a murdering whore, crying that she should be burnt. All sorts of insults. She was jostled on her horse. She nearly fell off.'

Kitty exclaimed again and Derry turned to look at her.

'Well, yes. I began to feel sorry for her myself. And none of the Lord stopped them. It was a real humiliation for a woman used to being praised and feted all her life. I had to run to keep up with her and the horsemen when we set off back. As she rode, her head was bowed but I could see her tears. She looked dreadful too. She had no royal clothes, just a few things she had had to borrow and they were mud spattered and didn't fit her properly. She looked tired and faint. It was worse when we got back to Edinburgh itself. The people must have heard she was coming and the streets were packed.'

'We heard the noise late last night. We thought it was the people cheering her return.'

'Oh, they weren't cheering. The people certainly turned out for her, but it was to shout at her, abuse her. There were so many people in the streets we had to slow down to get through. It must have been awful for her. They were calling her an adulteress, a murderess; they wanted her burned, drowned.'

Kitty was by now wiping her tears with the back of her hands. Her sniffles were drawing attention. There was little sympathy though from others about what had happened to the Queen. Will supposed that Kitty's tears came from her knowledge of what

Queen Mary had been like before all her disasters in Scotland. Her Majesty had probably been gracious and charming then, praising Kitty's delicious tarts and trying to lure her to come back to Scotland with her. Will could understand that, but back in France, Mary had been high in favour, rich and spoilt. She would have been used to having her own way all the time with no reason to complain. Will wasn't sure what he thought of the woman now. He just cared that Kitty was so distressed. He took her hand. And Derry paused to let her recover. But he was evidently eager to continue. There was more.

'The soldiers went back to the Castle or came here to the Palace. Mary was kept behind and then taken to a house on the High Street. I found out later that it belonged to the Provost, who supports the Lords. I don't know what happened in there but many in the crowd remained outside with me. They were still shouting. The women were worse than the men. Eventually they cleared off to their homes but I decided to stay. I slept in a doorway. It was a warm night.'

'Why?' asked Kitty. 'You have friends here who were worried about you when you didn't come back as expected.'

Derry turned again to look at her. He took her other hand now. Will was surprised to feel annoyed at that. Surely he wasn't jealous? He couldn't know that Derry was just appreciative of the fact that someone in his world cared for him in some small way. He hadn't had that since his sister died. But he was also enjoying telling his story, the feeling that he knew things that others didn't. Will did understand that, Derry's pleasure in being ahead of whatever was going on. He had first experienced that at Kirk o' Field. It irked him again.

'I'm used to sleeping outside. I've done a lot of that. It's easy in the summer. It wasn't raining. I stayed because I wanted to see what would happen next.'

'But weren't you hungry?' Will remembered that they had neither of them had anything to eat when they marched with the army. He remembered his own hunger.

'Oh, I had a bit of money and a pie seller came round. The pie wasn't as good as yours though. He looked at Kitty and annoyed Will again.

Kitty and Will looked at him with expectation. He seemed to have gathered some other listeners too, people sitting nearby who had overheard a story they didn't know either. They were leaning his way to hear more. It was strange. Will thought, that here was this boy who rarely spoke at all, now enjoying, relishing even, the audience he had before him

'Well, I was just across from the house where the Queen was. Guards had been placed outside. There were a few other people around when I woke up and I could hear gasps of surprise and the sound of windows opening. I looked up and it was Mary there, leaning forward from the shutters and out onto the street. What a sight! She sounded like some mad woman, crying and shrieking. Her hair had all fallen loose and was in tangles around her head. She was still in those dirty clothes but her bodice had come undone and her breasts were almost hanging out. It was unseemly. The abuse started up again from the crowd there but it seems a few people must have now begun to feel sorry for her. I did myself a bit. She looked so lost and abandoned'

Kitty patted Derry's hand. Her tears began again.

'Anyway, I think there must have been a meeting agreed upon for that morning as some of the lords' leaders began arriving. There was that Maitland. I recognised him.'

'He was the one who walked out on her and went over to the rebels,' Will looked across at Kitty and she nodded.

'Yes, he'd been her secretary and her mother's before her. What a traitor!'

'Well that explains why he pulled his hat down over his eyes and made out he hadn't seen her up there at the window. But two moments later, some arms came out and pulled her Majesty back into the room and shut the shutters. It was probably him who'd told them she was there. And even if he made out that he hadn't seen her, he must have heard her. She was shouting fit to burst. She even called his name.'

'So, is that when you came back here?

'No, I hung on a bit longer to see if I could find out the result of the meeting and sure enough that evening, the Queen was escorted back to Holyrood. On foot. Still in her dirty clothes. Her hair still tangled and disordered. There were hundreds of armed guards and the Lords followed behind. It was a pity to see her. And that banner was carried before her all the way.'

'The one with the baby Prince praying at his father's murdered corpse?' Will described it for Kitty. Derry nodded.

'So, she's here now?' said Kitty. 'At least she will have her maids to look after her again and they will make her something decent to eat in her own kitchen.'

Derry shook his head. 'No, she wasn't allowed to

stay here long enough. I was just thinking of going off to the great hall to get something to eat myself when she was brought out again. I followed them as carefully as I could and outside there were horses all saddled and ready to go. The Queen was helped onto one of them and then the group rode off. It looked like there were two women with them, chamber-maids perhaps. I have no idea where they went but I certainly couldn't follow horses.'

'Well, that looks like she is a prisoner to me,' said Will. 'You don't guard someone you have supposed-ly just set free. That's what they said they were fighting for. They claimed to be fighting for her honour, to free her from Bothwell, her husband's murderer. It doesn't look like that to me.'

Derry shifted his head towards those who had been listening to his story. He tried to speak with his eyes and Will understood the message. His story was one thing; many others had seen what had gone on but commenting on that now could be dangerous. He said nothing but it didn't stop him thinking. The

Queen was not an innocent, but she *was* the Queen. If the Lords were taking her off to be imprisoned somewhere, then that must be treason. It was high treason.

TWENTY-SIX

Will's brain was in tumult. He wanted to consider all the things he'd just heard from Derry, but everything just tumbled around his head and seemed to land upside down whenever he tried to find conclusions. And why did he need conclusions or opinions anyway? It was all none of his business. He was English and what could he do with any conclusions he came to? The likes of him were not supposed to have opinions. The Queen was gone, obviously a prisoner of those men who had proclaimed they were fighting in her best interests. And how stupid was it that when he had marched off with Derry to fight, he would have been fighting against her? Had he been on the wrong side according to any conclusions he came to? Had he been ready to die for a cause he barely understood?

But through all this muddle, even Will could see that the really important thing was the message that he had to go and see someone. What was that all about? The only clue he had was that the person who brought the message spoke with some sort of accent which Tom had thought was English. Will's heart had immediately lifted, thinking it could only be from his mother. Were she and Lord Randolph returned from wherever they'd been? But he hadn't seen her in the Great Hall. Had she sent a message? All he could do was wait until the man with the English accent arrived with his message again.

In the meantime, Bothwell had not reappeared and the rumour was that her Majesty had been imprisoned in Lochleven Castle which was on an island in the middle of a huge loch. To most people, that smacked of a prison from which Mary could not escape unless she could swim or row herself back to the mainland. And when Will heard that the castle belonged to the half-brother of the Lord Moray, he did have some sort of conclusion to his thinking. That man had been lurking in the background all the time, playing the Queen as it suited him. None of this was about Mary being restored to her throne. The only person being restored would be Moray as

Regent, the role he had been plotting to reclaim since his half-sister had arrived back from France. He had been patient and cunning, no doubt about that.

On the other hand, Mary had only herself to blame. She had made a disastrous marriage, cultivated the man Rizzio whom everyone hated, done nothing to eliminate the placards and them married another man, whom everyone thought was a murderer. She had not listened; she had pleased nobody but herself and look where that had led her. Maybe she couldn't help being ill but she had been a fool in every other respect. But, as Kitty regularly pointed out, she was still the Queen and Will was back to believing it was treason to treat her in this way. In any case, the Lords themselves had been dishonest, lying and scheming, according to the moment. Perhaps Moray would be the man they deserved? He would not be as weak as Mary had been, that was for sure.

Will kept his mouth shut and waited for the call from the messenger. If he had known who was calling him, he would have gone in search of the fellow. But he just kept quiet as a reward of 1,000 crowns was offered for the apprehension of Bothwell and the man was called officially to the Tolbooth to answer to the charges against him. He was given the statutory three weeks to appear but he never did, whereupon he was declared an outlaw and a rebel and all his honours, official roles and monies declared forfeit.

And then, just when Will was thinking the call had all been a mistake, it came, at the end of the day, when Will was unloading some of the roasted meats. Tom clicked a finger and called him over. The beautifully clothed manservant looked down at Will and turned on his heels. Will somehow knew he had to follow. Tom nodded. No permission had been sought but he gave it anyway. And Will followed. Not a word was said.

Gloomy corridor replaced gloomy corridor and after a while, Will felt that he had passed this way before. He was sure he was in a passage leading to

Lord Randolph's former rooms. His heart buzzed at the thought that his mother might be waiting for him behind a door just around the corner. He even recognised the door the manservant knocked at and invited him to pass through when an answer was given.

An older man, about the same age as Lord Randolph sat behind a desk opposite. It was not Lord Randolph and there was no sign of Will's mother either. Will felt his shoulders sag. The room was the same though.

'Come forward,' said the gentleman dismissing the manservant with a flick of his hand and addressing Will again, 'do you know who I am?'

'No, Sir'.

'I am Sir William Drury, Captain at Berwick and I came here to replace Lord Randolph, who has gone back to London. I'm more of a military man myself and will be going back to that position as soon as I can. I hope that Sir Nicholas Throckmorton will be able to carry out my role here then. I understand that you knew my Lord Randolph. Your mother is his housekeeper. Do I have the right boy?

'Yes, Sir.'

The man held up a piece of paper and fluttered it about as his evidence. Will would not have been able to verify what it was and could merely nod.

'Lord Randolph instructs me to take you to Berwick and from there ensure your transport to London. He will send someone to meet you at the end of your London journey. I understand that you will be able to stay with Lord Randolph. I do not know what other plans he has for you. I am informed by him that you mother is ill and that she wishes to see you.'

Will's shoulders rose and fell within minutes. He was going to London, everything he had always hoped for, and then his mother was ill, which turned his excitement instantly into something quite other.

He looked earnestly at Sir Drury. 'How ill is my mother?'

'I know nothing of that.' Sir Drury looked upon Will with indifference. 'I will take you to Berwick myself as I need to be there next week. I will send again to you with the day and time and a meeting place. You must make sure you are ready to leave.'

There was a long pause as he sniffed the air and applied a kerchief to his nose. 'If I am to travel with you personally, I need you to be cleaner than you are now. My Lord Randolph has sent me some money for you to dress yourself more appropriately. If you smell as you do now, I will have to leave you behind. My stomach will not be able to support your aroma. Berwick is not far, but it is far enough for you to turn my insides.'

Sir Drury took a small package from his desk and handed it to Will. Will assumed it was the money and shoved it down the front of his ragged shirt. It was not safe to be seen with money in his world.

Sir Drury shuddered with distaste as the money slid between Will's soiled shirt and his body.

'Thank you, Sir,' said Will bowing. He wasn't sure if that was what should be done under such circumstances.

'Don't spend all that on clothes. You will need to make provision for your journey. It is for you to pay for your overnight accommodation at the stopping places and for any food and drink you require. Do I make myself clear?'

'Yes, Sir. Will I be coming back here?'

'If you mean back to Edinburgh, I have no idea. That is not my concern. It will be for Lord Randolph to decide. You may go.'

Will bowed again and backed out of the room. As he did so, the manservant came in to say 'your young man is here again, Sir.' Sir Drury nodded 'send him in then.'

Will backed out further and as he did so, he almost fell into Derry, who was standing outside. The two lads looked at one another but there was no time to say anything. The faces spoke their mutual aston-ishment as Derry was ushered into the room Will had just vacated and Will was shoved away down the corridor. Will clutched the package to his chest and when he had recovered from his surprise, it did occur to him to tiptoe back and listen at the door. He decided against it. He wanted to get his package hidden before anyone saw him with it.

There was no-one in the kitchen. He counted the money in the package. It seemed an outrageous amount but probably wasn't. He had no idea what costs the journey would entail. He added it to the much smaller amount he had in his hidden collection in the wall near the turnspit and then sat in his former spit place and stared into the fire. Whatever was wrong with his mother, it must surely be serious. Lord Randolph would never have needlessly paid for his return if it didn't matter. He wanted to be with her, but at the moment of his having the possibility of leaving this place he had called a stinkpot or some such for so long, he now felt his stomach churning. It wasn't just his mother, it was the leaving itself. Here, he was warm and he looked into the flames again. He had a fixed shelter and food without worry. Here, he had a place where he knew people. He had friends. He had even been promoted, if chopping vegetables for the pottage constituted a move upwards from turning the spit. Well, it did in his world. He wasn't worried about the loss of the Queen. He didn't think she would be coming back and the likes of Lord Moray wouldn't be worrying about the lowlife of the Palace. He wouldn't lose his place. Except he *was* losing his place. He was losing it now.

How long would it take for him to get to London and could he come back to what he'd left behind? Derry had only been away a few days and he had been downgraded. Water carrier? Will didn't want that. But he had to go. He didn't want to, but if his mother had called for him, he did want to.

And then there were the friends he would be leaving behind. Strangely, it was Kitty who came first into his mind. They had just been getting to know one another but he knew he looked forward to seeing her every day. He thought she was beautiful and just sitting talking to her was a joy; she was so easy to talk to, but he loved listening to how she spoke too. She was older than he was. She probably wasn't interested in him and perhaps he was just being childish? He couldn't help himself. He wasn't too worried about anyone else. They could be replaced but Kitty …?

And lastly there was Derry. He couldn't call him a friend. He wasn't to be trusted. He was still behaving secretly after all they'd gone through together. Who knew what he was up to? Even now he would be with Sir Drury. What was that about? The manservant had called him 'your young man' as if Derry was already known to Drury. Will had scarcely heard of Drury before. How had Derry come to know the man so well?

Will turned as the kitchen door heaved open and there was Derry.

'Ah, I thought I might find you here,' Derry said.

Will didn't reply but he was thinking. Of course Derry would find him wherever he was; he always knew how to find people; and yet nobody knew how to find him.

Perhaps Derry saw Will's scowl? 'Sir Drury told me that you will be leaving. He told me about your mother. Sorry to hear that she is ill.'

Was there anything Derry didn't know? Resentment was bitter in Will's mouth. Could he have no privacy? And he still didn't want to speak. Derry was oblivious.

'I see Drury regularly. I give him information about what is happening in the Palace. I don't have to say much but he gives me a coin each time. Very welcome!' He tossed what was probably his most recent coin through the sir.

'Ah, so you're the spy.' Will's voice rattled with spite.

'Yes, it wasn't Jennet as everyone thought. It was me. I just let people think what they like.'

Will looked Derry up and down. There was nothing he found to like about the lad. His dislike must have been obvious.

'Actually, I did help you to rescue Bessie. I did tell you where she might be found.' Of course Derry knew what Will was thinking.

'Yes, but you did leave us to think badly of her. She was probably just working alongside her family. She did not betray Bessie.'

'But they were supporters of Bothwell … her father and her uncle, the Ormistons. And it's the lords who pay me. They're searching for Darnley's murderers now. I'm being paid for my help with that.'

'Are you being paid by the lords who were part of the conspiracy to murder Darnley? They are murderers too aren't they? Or do you only betray the little people? The people of no consequence?'

Derry shrugged. 'I just look after myself. I do what I can at my level, I can't spy on the lords. They'd soon get rid of me.'

'You're a lavvy bampot,' exclaimed Will. It was the best he could do. He wasn't even sure what it meant. He'd heard it amongst the solders on the way to Carberry Hill. It helped how he felt now.

Derry just laughed. 'That sounds funny coming out of your mouth with your English ways. And he repeated it with his Scottish accent 'You're a lavvy bampot; you're a lavvy bampot.'

Will got up and moved towards the door. 'Perhaps you'll allow me to be the first to tell Tom tomorrow that I'm leaving. Can you contain yourself for that long?' And without turning back again, he left.

TWENTY-SEVEN

Will had just a week to get himself ready. He managed to find better clothes in his chest and bought himself a pair of good quality second hand shoes. Kitty cut his hair to his scalp so that he felt almost naked and she brought him some twigs from a plant she called Rosemary which she found in the Palace gardens. She said he should use them to clean his teeth. She also provided the soap again which she kept in the kitchen and which he had last used on the 'boys'. Bessie made him some linen underwear to take with him and told him to change every few days.

Will felt he was being 'mothered by them all. It was all rather too personal for him. He wished he'd never told them what Sir Drury had said about his appearance and his cleanliness. Will asked Tom if he could buy the knife he had borrowed from the kitchens several times. He was nervous about the part of the journey he would have to undertake on his own. Tom gave it to him instead. When at last he told them that he would be leaving the next day and wouldn't see them again, he struggled to keep his back straight and his head up. Kitty produced some of her pies and John had organised some good quality bread for him from the bakery. It was all he could do to carry it with him as he went to the courtyard to wait for Sir Drury. Kitty was there before him.

'What are you doing here?'

'We couldn't let you go alone. As if you were friendless.'

'I didn't want anyone to come. I didn't want to get upset.'

'It's only me. Tom gave me permission to send all our best wishes.' She didn't add that she had been the only person who had asked to go.

She held out a hand to him as Lord Drury's carriage arrived around the corner. There wasn't time for Will to do much more than take her hand in return, before giving his things to the footman who had descended to collect them. Kitty snatched a moment to kiss Will's cheek as he climbed into the carriage. Sir Drury was glaring at him as he sat down. Will grabbed her hand and brought it to his lips.

'I can't read or write but I will always remember you,' he shouted as the horses started off.

Sir Drury was now laughing at him.

'Ah, the tender little sweetheart. There's plenty more of those in London.'

Will tried to smile back but it was the last thing he wanted to do. He was uncomfortable in his change of clothes, especially in the uncomfortable new shoes. He hope there wouldn't be much walking to do. There was silence for a long time until Sir Drury began with his questions.

'I understand you work alongside Derry. He has told me about you. And what do you think of the spectacular goings-on in Edinburgh over the last few months? You can tell me now you're leaving.'

'Is that safe, Sir? One of the kitchen staff was arrested for speaking out against Lord Bothwell'.

'Ah, Bothwell. It's safe to say what you like about

him now. You'll never see him again. None of us will. He's fled to the Orkneys and is trying to get a ship to Norway or Denmark. His support has all but fallen away.'

'And Her Majesty, my Lord?'

'She won't be coming back either. Even if she escapes, she has no followers.'

'So what will happen to Scotland without her?'

''The Lord Moray will be made Regent again shortly and he will rule until the little Prince is old enough to do so. And he has the approval of our Queen Bess. You needn't worry about Scotland.'

It was just as Will had predicted. He felt pleased with himself and couldn't feel much compassion for Mary, Darnley or Bothwell, and he now said so, feeling quite daring and outspoken.

'So, who murdered Darnley?' asked Drury.

'I don't know but I know who will be punished for it. All the lowly people. Those lords who had a part in the planning will talk their way out of it or disappear to their lands. You'll see.'

'You seem very sure,'

'It's always the same. We both know that.'

Drury said nothing knowing the lords were already going after the common folk and Will was wondering whether they would catch Jennet's family. He didn't know how he felt about that. He supposed that they were part of what he had called the lowly people.

'And was her Majesty part of the conspiracy against Darnley?'

'I think so.' Will paused, wondering if he ought to continue. But he had thought so hard about all this over the last weeks that he couldn't resist the chance to speak. 'I think she knew about the plan. I think she lured her husband back to Edinburgh from Glasgow with the promise of forgiveness and his marriage rights again. She was not opposed to lying when it suited her. She wouldn't have wanted Darley back in her bed.. He was ugly and foul smelling. He was due to return to the Palace the next day and so he was killed the night before. It all makes sense.

She had a wedding to go to. That was her excuse for leaving him.'

It was strange. It was if Will's mind was clarifying as he left Edinburgh behind. He had never felt so sure about what he thought.

'And Bothwell?'

'Ah, I don't know about that. He was surely involved in the murder but as for his influence with the Queen, he was probably a bully who took advantage of her when she was weak and ill.'

Will thought sadly of Bessie who was just beginning to recover from her abduction when he left. Bessie had had proof of Bothwell's brutal behaviour with her cousin.

'You are wise beyond your years,' Drury said. 'One should always talk to the lower people if one wants to know anything.'

'Is that why you employ Derry?' Will ignored the fact that the man was referring to him as the lower people. He no longer cared.

Well he was just pursuing money. He does work

hard though.'

'I will never trust him again. He let an innocent girl in our kitchen be suspected instead of him.'

Will now wondered if Derry knew all about Lord Randolph and his mother. Knowing Derry he would.

'But that is what makes him a good spy.'

'But not a good friend. And if he got caught and punished, you would disown him, wouldn't you? You wouldn't care. '

'I expect I wouldn't. He's not important.'

They arrived in Berwick sooner than Will had anticipated. He had intended looking out at the countryside as they travelled but had done very little of that. He had seen the sea at one point and marvelled at its size. He looked around now as he stepped down from the carriage. He liked what he saw. The town was small, bustling and cleaner than Edinburgh. Yes, there were poor people but they didn't seem to be as pitiable as those he'd left behind. But there would probably be nasty parts somewhere hidden in the back streets. There always were.

Drury said he had somewhere else to go after his journey but he took Will to the coaching inn and informed them at a desk that this young lad with him was wanting to go to London. Could they recommend anyone who was going in that direction?

As he listened, Will was realising that going to London was not quite as easy as he had imagined. He didn't know quite what he'd imagined but it wasn't begging for rides. How would he know which direction he had to take in his rides? He was relieved that he had at least got that knife from the kitchen.

A voice came in from the ale room.

'I'm going to Alnwick in about an hour. It's south. You can go on from there.'

It sounded a bit vague to Will but Drury seemed to think it a good idea. Perhaps he merely wanted to get rid of the lad? Will wasn't his responsibility after all.

Drury argued a price and took the money off Will.

'Always get a price first,' he advised and then wished him well and disappeared.

Will sat outside and ate one of Kitty's pies. He didn't want to miss the carter leaving. It was a good pie, but it upset him thinking of Kitty and the others. He felt more alone than he had ever been before. And to think he had complained about his lot back at the Palace.

The carter came out, clearly reeling after his drink.

He led Will along the road and they climbed into an old uncovered cart. What a difference after Drury's carriage! Will had not appreciated it at the time. That had been almost stately, with upholstered seats even if the leather had been well-worn. Will now sat on cheap wooden boards with a thin and shabby cushion to protect him from the potholes and jutting stones of the road. And the carter found every one. It could only have been worse if it had been raining. At least July was warm.

'I'm not going right into Alnwick', the carter said after they had been traveling for some time. There hadn't been much conversation. The man had been dozing in his ale. 'You'll have to walk along the

road aways and there's an inn you can stay in overnight.'

Fine,' said Will, hiding his dismay, 'and where do I
need to aim for next if I'm going to London?'

'I reckon Morpeth or Newcastle. There may be
somewhere in between. I don't know.'

Will found the inn, after the carter turned off, but
saw beyond it an untidy farm building where he decided he would sleep the night. He was worried
about his money and wanted to make sure he didn't
run short. He would set off as early as he could in
the morning and see where he could get to from
Alnwick.

He got to a small place called Wide Open which he
was told was only a few miles from Newcastle. He
liked the name and decided to treat himself to some
proper food in the inn there. He was hoping the innkeeper would be 'wide open' in his honesty. He was,
and had a son in law who was going to Newcastle
the next day. In fact he was going to Durham, which
he told Will would be even further south for him.

Durham's cathedral stood tall even before they were near the town. And then it seemed an age to the town itself. Will was glad they hadn't stopped in Newcastle. It had looked even more depressing than Edinburgh. Will had shared the rest of his pies and bread with the son in law, a chirpy fellow called Arthur. It was a relief to get rid of the pies as he was worried about gut rot after so many days. And the bread was hard, though edible when dipped in the universal pottage. Will was sorry to part from Arthur and promised to visit the family in Wide Open if he ever passed that way again. He didn't think he ever would. He had not realised how far away London was. How could he ever afford to travel in the opposite direction? He vaguely remembered travelling to Scotland in Lord Randolph's carriage so many years ago. That had not seemed so arduous..

Will started walking out of Durham but soon regretted his previous enthusiasm for the wild, open country, as no matter how lovely the scenery, the agony of his shoes began to distract him. He took them off and then regretted that too, as the bare ground was worse. He had seen people walking easy and barefoot in Edinburgh but it wasn't as comfortable as they had made it seem. Perhaps they had grown up barefoot, whereas he hadn't? He was sitting by the wayside tying up his boots again and wondering what he could stuff down them to protect his heels when he was overtaken by another cart.

'Whire ye goin to, lad?' The voice was cheery and friendly and the owner not much older than Will himself.

I'm trying to get to London.'

'My, yons a lang ways to go.'

'Could you take me some of the way?. Are you going south? I have a little money.'

'I can tek yous to Sedgefield and then maybees you cud get on fro' there. If yous can get to Boroughbridge, I unnerstan thes a coach to Loddon fro there,'

'Oh, please. Thank you.' Will climbed onto the cart before the young man could change his mind.

He didn't actually care which way he was going but it had to be better than walking in those boots.

The young man, George, and Will had a conversation of sorts as they trundled along. They didn't understand each other much but there was a lot of laughter in trying to. In Sedgefield George invited Will into the local inn. Will thought he said that he knew someone who lived in Boroughbridge. Whoever it was, he wasn't there. Maybe Will hadn't understood properly? However, he got another offer to Darlington which the speaker said was on the way to Boroughbridge. Will caught the doubt in George's voice when the offer was made and then the negative look in his eyes. The offer was repeated and Will, didn't know what to do. He was trying to find the words to decline when George spoke.

'Nay, it ull be fine. I'll tek him on to my friend's 'ouse and then he can get to Boroughbridge in the morning.'

Outside again, George said 'I woudna trust yon fellow. He'll truss you up for to tek your money. Or wurse. I'll tek you further on and yous can sleep in a barn till he's gun.'

That was fine with Will, and, when he dropped him off, George wouldn't take any money. He said he was just pleased to have had the company. Will was pleased how the journey was going, thinking of how much money he must have been saving. It made him feel more secure. He was frightened of the tales he'd heard about London and the cost of everything there. But then, Will's grumbling stomach reminded him that he'd had nothing to eat since he'd been dropped. But he realised that he was now stuck in the barn. He didn't dare leave it. He would have to starve until the morning.

Asking at the inn in Boroughbridge, where he'd filled the gaping hole in his stomach, he discovered that there was a coach to London as George had said. The innkeeper said it left every Monday.

'What day is it today?' Will had no idea. His head had lost the path of the days.

'Friday. Do you want to stay here until then?'

Could he afford it? Three nights? He'd saved a lot already sleeping in barns but he was still worried about London. He had finally woken to the fact that Lord Randolph could hardly meet him in London. How would he know when Will would be arriving? Or where? It had probably been something Drury had said to waylay Will's fears. And it had worked.

The innkeeper looked at him and must have seen the struggle in Will's head. 'I can give you a pallet upstairs, sharing with whoever else turns up.'

What choice did Will have? He had been seen arriving and might now be a target for people like the man George had feared in Durham. Will accepted the offer and the pottage and bread each evening that went with it. The pottage was thin and lukewarm, but he ate it. Then he sought out the upstairs room which was exactly that, just a room with some pallets stacked up against a wall. Two pallets had already been set out so that Will knew he would be sharing the place with two others. Perhaps they were the men he had seen eating pottage at another table downstairs? He set his own pallet well away from them underneath the window. He had some idea of jumping out of it, if necessary. He was as wary as he'd ever been. It was as well it was a warm night as there was no sign of a blanket. He would manage.

He was vaguely aware of the other men coming in later but feigned full sleep and when he woke in the morning, they were gone. But the pallets were still in place. Did that mean they were coming back? Could he risk leaving his bag when he went out for the day? He decided he would. There was nothing of value in it. Before he'd set out from Edinburgh he had wrapped his money up around his midriff with some strips of cloth Bessie had found for him. Getting it out whenever needed was a struggle and had to be private, but he kept a little in his pocket too.

Two days to mooch around in Boroughbridge was a challenge but there was a market where he could set himself up again with food and there was a river where he could wash. Otherwise, there were just sheep and lots of those. The sheep looked at him steadfastly, as they munched and ground their teeth. That's all they did, that and drop their waste every-where.

On the second evening when Will went up to sleep, he discovered that his bag had been gone through. It wasn't really a bag. He had just packed his things into a huge piece of cloth and knotted them together. He had left his chest in Kitty's keeping. He had tried to give it to her but she had insisted that she could not accept. It would be there for him on his return. Did that mean she was hoping he would return? It gave him an opening if he ever did. His thoughts had often dwelt on that as he journeyed.

There was nothing missing but he knew the bag had been tampered with. It was not where he had left it and his knot was different. What to do? Anyone could have come up here during the day, not just the men he shared with ... the innkeeper, his wife, any of his servants or the customers. Did he want to start accusations? He was alarmed that those who had interfered with his things must know now that any money he had would be on his person. He hardly slept that night and had his knife in his hand.

He was the only traveller when he stepped into the coach good and early the next morning, but an elderly couple arrived later and during the journey, various people got on or left. The two men from the upper room did not appear. The relief was enormous. Were they just passing journeymen working in the area?

Now began a long and laborious journey, broken only by various overnight stops and changes of horses. The carriage was better than the carts, dry at least, but not by much. The roads rose and fell, full of enormous holes filled occasionally with rubble and animal dirt which shot up into the carriage from time to time from under the wheels and filled the carriage with outrage, dirt and unwanted smells. Sometimes, Will felt he could walk faster and with more comfort in spite of his shoes.

It was a joy every evening to step down from the

monotony, noise and discomfort of the thing. Will wanted nothing more when they stopped than to eat and sleep. He was told at Grantham that the inn where he slept had been the place where King Richard the Third had signed Buckingham's death warrant. He neither knew or cared who either of these had been. What he did welcome was the news that there would only be one more stop, Stamford, before reaching London.

The journey terminated at a place called Smithfield, where there seemed to be more animals than people. The approach to London had been wondrous, so many things to see. They passed herds of cattle on the way, the animals being harried forward into huge fenced pens as they neared Smithfield. There were sheep and birds that Will had known more intimately on his spit than in real life.

It seemed a strange place to finish up, amongst animals, and he was lost in the bustling madness of it all. He had no idea what to do next. All he had was a vague address and he was looking for somewhere to sit to think out his next move, when he felt his sleeve tugged. He was instantly alert and his hand reaching for his knife. Looking down, he saw a filthy hand clutching at his jacket and then he saw the hand's owner, an equally filthy urchin.

TWENTY-EIGHT

The urchin grinned at him.

'Are you William Randolph? I've been sent to meet you.'

Will was suspicious. 'What if I am? How could you possibly know when to meet me, and where?'

'Lord Randolph is paying me to meet each coach that comes in and look out for a boy of about your age. I get so much for each day I wait. I've been coming for over a week now. We were beginning to wonder if you were coming some other way.'

'And now that you've met me?'

'So you *are* William Randolph? I can't be taking the wrong person away'.

'And where would you be taking him to?'

'To Lord Randolph's house. St Peter's Hill.' Which was exactly the address Will had in his head. He had a street name too and asked for it from the lad.

'Oh, that's easy, Sir. Thames Street, after our big river here. You can't forget it.' That was correct too.

'Well, come on, then. Let's go! Can we walk it?'

'Oh, I can, Sir, but can you? I'll carry your things for you. Follow me. If you get tired, we can get a cab. Well, we can if you've got some money.'

It was further than Will had anticipated but his shoes must have been getting easier and he was certainly glad to be free of the lumbering stagecoach. When the lad… he said his name was Jemmy … finally rapped on an impressive wooden door in an impressive street of impressive houses, Will was surprised when a frosty-looking middle aged woman answered it. Somehow, he had been expecting Lord Randolph himself or perhaps his mother ... she was the housekeeper after all and her absence sent ripples of anxiety through his body. It was the right house though and the woman gave Jemmy a coin and took Will through a gloomy panelled corridor to a bleak back room where Lord Randolph sat, almost as if in waiting. He waved Will to a chair at the other side of the fireplace, except that there was no fire. The room was, therefore, chilly in its welcome but

Will sat dutifully, the woman left and Will remained with the silent Lord Randolph. Lord Randolph had never been much of a talker. Well, not to Will anyway, but he had always been smiling and kind. There was no sign of Will's mother. Lord Randolph was not smiling now. Will felt anothe ripple of uncomfortable anxiety flow through his body.

'I'm glad you've arrived safely, Will. Drury wrote telling me that you had set off.'

Will nodded and mumbled. He didn't know what to say. He was fearing the worst now, but wasn't even sure what the worst was.

'My mother?' he said, without expression.

'Yes, I'm sorry. I sent for you as soon as we realised that she was ill. She wanted to see you.' He was silent for a long time and then just repeated himself. 'I'm so sorry.'

'She is dead then?' asked Will. It sounded brutal but he couldn't have borne a long drawn out story. He somehow knew without being told. 'I haven't been able to get here in time?'

'No, and because it's a hot summer, we couldn't delay the funeral.'

'I have missed that as well?'

Will fought not to give way to tears. He felt he had to be strong for whatever reason. But he had to wipe his eyes as if he had a speck in one of them. It was a pretence that Lord Randolph easily saw through..

'What did she die of?' he asked eventually, though it no longer mattered. He was alone and bereft again. This would be his life now. He had come such a long way to find out that nothing had changed.

'We're not sure. At first we thought it was the sleeping sickness but there hasn't been any of that around for a time. And then she admitted that she had felt unwell for some while but hadn't said anything. You know what she was like.'

Will knew. She would have battled to the end.

'And now we think she had a growth of some kind. There was nothing anyone could have done. We tried all the usual … cupping, leeches, purges. We consulted a supposedly wise woman, who prescribed herbs and other things to be taken, but all in vain. She lapsed into her final sleep and the end was as peaceful as it could be.'

'How long ago?'

'Oh, not long. Only a few days ago for the funeral. I expected you sooner.'

Will was thinking of Drury. He had dallied after the first message. He had taken Will to Berwick when it suited him. Will could have set off earlier. He could at least have been with his mother at the end and now he would never see her again. He cursed Drury for his thoughtlessness.

'But you must be hungry. And tired. Forgive me. I will show you to your room. It's the one you used to sleep in when you lived here. Do you remember being here? It was a long time ago.'

'No, not really. I would have been lost without that young boy you sent to look after me. Thank you for that.'

'I have also got some things to go over with you. Your mother left you a package. But all that can wait until tomorrow. I will send some food up to your room and then you don't have to be bothered with anything until the morning. Come down when you are ready.'

There was just enough light left for Will to see out of the window of his room and he did now recognise the garden he had played in as a child, even though the trees which had appeared enormous at the time, now loomed even larger. It seemed a lifetime ago and yet he had still not even come of age. He could scarcely believe that it was the usual pottage and bread which the housekeeper brought for him. The bread was warm with melting butter but it was much like what he had been eating for more than a week, eating all his life or so it felt. But he was safe and proud that he'd made this journey alone. He felt he could do anything now. He was only sad that he had been too late and he blamed Drury again for that. It was only when sleep overtook him that his mother slipped from his thoughts.

In the morning he wanted to ask to see where his

mother had been buried and was then excited later about seeing what she had left for him. He expected little tokens of her affection over the years, perhaps some of his playthings which she had kept. He also needed to think about what his future would be, to hear what Lord Randolph might have to say about that. Lord Randolph brought out a wooden box.

'Your mother left this for you. I have no idea what's in it but think you should look at it on your own in your own time so that your remembrances can be private. I can, though, tell you about the more public things you need to know.' And he passed over some papers. It was hard to take in some of the details but at the end, Will understood that his mother had amassed quite a sum of money that would now come to him.

'I can explain how she did it,' began Randolph at Will's astonishment. 'You know that she lived all her life with me and looked after me in everything. She had modest wages but she didn't need them. This was her home and she made food for both of us. The cost of it came through to me. She needed to buy nothing but her clothes and she spent little on those. She mostly wore the household clothes I paid for. She liked to be plain and simple. She was no follower of fashion. You know that. The gifts she was given were put in this box. You'll find them there I expect. You'll find that some of them will be worth a bit too. There's a lovely brooch I gave her one Christmas, which she wore on the day and which I rarely saw thereafter. She had the occasional admirer too when she was younger and received tokens from them. But she wasn't interested. What she did like was the garden, the flowers, the shrubs. I learnt to give her plants as presents as we grew used to one another.'

Lord Randolph paused, as if remembering, and again, Will wondered about the relationship between them. Lord Randolph had never married and it was obvious he had thought much of his mother. People didn't usually give an expensive gift like a valuable brooch to an ordinary servant. The new housekeeper, the frosty woman whom he had met at the door, had taken over his mother's old room and so he could not look for clues there. It was interesting, though, that the woman was, in Will's estimation, quite unattractive. She was probably even older than his mother. Lord Randolph was not interested in a replacement in that sense. Will just had to accept that he would never know. He certainly didn't dare to ask.

Lord Randolph came out of his wistfulness and seemed surprised to see Will still sitting there.

'You used to be a sensible boy. I can see you haven't changed and so I advise you to think carefully about what you do with this money. I have no idea what your plans for the future might be. Do you have any?'

Will tried to think but he had never had any money to make plans with. It had never occurred to him. He shook his head.

'No, Sir. I wanted to leave Edinburgh, but now I miss it and the friends I had there.'

'Why did you want to leave Edinburgh?'

'Because it is a filthy place and the people suffer so much in their poverty. The richer people behave badly and are always fighting one other. They can't even agree in their worship of God. It's a brutal place.'

Lord Randolph laughed.

'And you think London might be better? I can assure you that it is not. There are disparities of wealth wherever you go and there is intrigue between people everywhere too. You will see this as you grow older. Look, you can stay here and make this your home if you wish. But I will not be here most of the time, as I have been posted to Russia and will be leaving soon.'

'Russia?' It was another world. It was beyond Will's imagination.

'Yes, I am going on behalf of some English merchants. They expect me to organise trade deals for them at the court of King Ivan. I think their kings are called Tsars. So that would be Tsar Ivan.'

Will was still stupefied and yet he knew he didn't want to stay in an empty house with Mrs 'Frump', the housekeeper. However, there was one thing he did want.

'I would like to learn to read and write,' he announced boldly. If I can stay here for a short while. If my mother and I had learned, we could have written to one another.' And he thought further. If he learned, he could write now to Kitty, even if she couldn't read what he'd put. He didn't think she could read but she could ask someone to read for her.

'That could be easily arranged. I will sort a tutor to come to the house to teach you as soon as possible. I have been remiss in not organising that for you in the past. It will be at my expense. And then you will be able to write to me too.' He laughed, pleased with himself.

'Now, is there anything else? What would you like to do in London? And perhaps we can think about a job for you? What are you interested in? What are you good at? What are your talents?

Will's face grew dull. He was accustomed to thinking of himself as having no talents and began dismally 'I can't do much.' Then he thought further. Perhaps there were things he could do but did anyone value them? 'I can cook all kinds of meat and poultry, set the spit up, you know, and know when to baste them. I can serve them properly. I know about sauces and vegetables. Oh, and pottage … can't forget that! I think I could make that with my eyes closed.'

Lord Randolph clapped his hands, which was a rare moment of joviality for him.

'And do you like doing all that?'

'I would if I could organise it all myself. I like going to the stores to select what to cook. It's just so hot. The spit in the Palace is enormous.'

'Well, we must find an eating house here in London and see what you think. And perhaps you could make pottage for me? I don't think it's one of Mrs. Fry's strengths.'

They laughed together, Will thinking the name Fry went well with 'Frumpy'. He couldn't remember Lord Randolph laughing much in his childhood. Maybe it was because Will was older now or perhaps his mother's death had raised regrets about the past in general. It was as well that he was off to Russia soon, as Lord Randolph would be lonely in that huge house with just Frumpy Fry. As would he himself if he stayed there. But what else could he do?

TWENTY-NINE

There was more money from his mother than Will would ever have expected. He suspected that Lord Randolph had perhaps added to the sum himself, for whatever reason. He tried to pay back what he'd spent in travelling from Edinburgh but Lord Randolph wouldn't hear of it and instead ensured that Will bought some clothes which actually fitted him.

The weather was still very dry so that free evenings were spent in the garden his mother had loved and the talk was often of Lord Randolph's time in Scotland. He was scathing about Queen Mary but seemed to have quite liked Bothwell until Will, pleased with his awareness, filled in the gaps in his knowledge. Randolph admitted to taking his own Queen's side in everything. Good Queen Bess was so much higher in worthiness in his opinion. Will was inclined to agree, though he did think that Mary must be more beautiful. He had never seen Queen Elizabeth.

Nothing had been decided for Will's future, though

he did now have an English tutor. He didn't find it as easy as he had imagined. He had to struggle and would have abandoned it all but for Lord Randolph pushing him forward. He persevered and if someone wrote something out for him, he could copy it neatly in his own hand so that he felt as if he were writing himself.

But he didn't dare write to Kitty. He thought of her a grcat deal, especially when he was in the garden on his own when Lord Randolph had to go in to deal with a visitor. His mother had been happy here and happy with Lord Randolph too. That seemed important. All the wrestling for power he had seen in Scotland had influenced his thinking. Randolph had introduced him to important people in London and he sensed the same restlessness and hunger for advancement in them. It wasn't for him and maybe working in the kitchens had not been so bad after all. It was warm and dry and people were mostly friendly. He would have liked a bit more responsibility though and would have stepped willingly into Tom

Croft or John Parlick's shoes, but they had years of service before them. There was no chance of that. As for people, there was a chatty little parlour maid here, but she fussed too much and her silly eagerness to please began to irritate him. He so missed Kitty's quietness, her common sense and her beautiful fingers. But how could he say he was lonely when there was a heaving market down the road, any number of alehouses and even a theatre which Randolph had taken him to on several occasions?

The eating houses Lord Randolph took him to ranged from elegant parlours with stylish furniture to grubby rooms with scratched chairs, soiled tablecloths and overfriendly waitresses who belied the real purpose of the establishment. They didn't eat in the latter. They just looked in at the doorway for Will to confirm his no thank you.

It was probably one of the last days of the warm autumn when Lord Randolph sat with Will in the garden and asked him what he'd made of London. Will had now seen the hovels some of the population lived in. He had seen the jostling for power amongst the higher ranks and he had seen the filth in the streets. There were certainly elegant buildings and elegant people to go with them but they made Will uncomfortable and he could scarcely believe it when he thought that actually Edinburgh might be his preference.

'And the eating houses?' asked Lord Randolph.

'I like the simpler ones best. You can see the food is well cooked and that everything is clean. I don't like the fussiness of the expensive ones. You're pay-ing for that and the food is no better.'

'Well, I've been thinking about you. I was wonder-ing whether that might be the life for you.'

'You mean working in one of those?'

'Yes, but not as you're thinking. I was meaning you could have one of those yourself.'

Will's face flushed red in shock. 'You're not serious are you? I couldn't afford it.'

'You could if you started off by renting premises. You'd have to buy all the equipment at first, of

course, but afterwards, if you drew in enough customers, who knows? What do you think? It's just an
idea.'

But it was an idea which grew. Will watered it and
nursed it in the sunshine. As autumn grew to an end,
he kept it out of the wind and pinched out the growing point to make it bushy. Lord Randolph had
planted a wonderful seed and it sprouted forth in
Will's head until he had so many additional ideas of
his own.

He thought of Kitty and she began to slide into his
plans. It seemed to be where she belonged. Could he
get her to come and work with him? Probably not,
but what if he tried? She would be reluctant to leave
a reliable post for the precarious one he could offer,
but once thought of, it wouldn't leave him. He
thought of her pies, the delicious pastries she con-
cocted. Perhaps he could get her to make those for
his eating house? But if they were both making the
food, who would serve the customers? Derry flashed
into his mind but he quickly flushed him out again.

No thank you. And where would this eating place be? Would it be here in London or would he go back to Edinburgh or even settle somewhere else?

Will's main question was left unanswered as time passed and Lord Randolph began preparing to leave for Russia. Will had wanted to ask Lord Randolph about his parentage but he had to leave that question hanging in the air. He was just too embarrassed to raise it.

Lord Randolph left in mid-January and then Will found himself rattling round in the house with Mrs Fry, Maggie, the fussy maid, and a man called Mr. Williams, whom Randolph had engaged to oversee the house during his absence. Lord Randolph had seemed to think a man was necessary to maintain the building and protect everyone, but Will wasn't happy. He found Mr Williams overbearing and resentful of him, presumably for not doing a job of any kind or contributing to the household expenses. Williams made Mrs Fry his ally and the two of them regularly made snide remarks and failed to talk to him.

When Will had suffered the prevailing silence for long enough, he went out one morning and bought himself a stage ticket for Berwick. He'd discovered such a coach existed when he'd bought his previous ticket in Boroughbridge. That was another grudge he had against Drury. Drury may even have known that the coach went from Edinburgh all the way to London but the ticket for Berwick now was an instinctive thing for Will. If Moray was going to be ruling in Scotland, Will didn't want any part of it. He felt Berwick would be safer. It was in England and he was English after all.

Will packed his things, including his mother's box, in a newly bought proper leather travelling bag for this journey. He left poor Maggie to her fate with Mrs. Fry and Mr. Williams and took the stage from Smithfield. The ride was as uncomfortable as ever but took even longer because of the icy roads and poor weather. He was cold and had to go as far as Stamford to find a decent woollen blanket he could buy. He used it thereafter for the overnight stops. He felt he was treated more courteously this time and guessed it was because of his better quality clothes. It confirmed how he thought the world worked.

He looked out for Arthur in Wide Open but didn't search him out. There was no time. In Berwick, he found himself some basic lodgings and went walking around the town. He wanted to 'feel' the place as a possible location for an eating house, but he had no real idea how to judge. He didn't really want to go back to Edinburgh. He still felt the danger, the filth, the treachery of the city. He found a few buildings in various states of condition which might serve. There would be a lot of work. He was wondering again if he could afford it. He wanted somewhere where he could live on the premises, a fireplace he could adapt to install a spit and a nearby source of water. Randolph had brought a friend round to his house before he left for Russia. The man was able to advise Will on how much he ought to be paying for premises and how to argue for the best price, not just for the shop but for everything he would need with it. The man advised that property in Edinburgh would probably be cheaper than in London but Will was now calculating that Berwick might be cheaper again. As for his workers, if Tom Croft could go around the Edinburgh slums and select a few capable boys, Will reckoned he could do the same in Berwick. He settled for nothing, engaged no-one and bought not a single piece of equipment, but he felt that he would now be able to go forward.

THIRTY

The young man who stepped out into Edinburgh was a different person to the young lad who had started work in the Palace kitchens so long ago. The city hadn't changed, but Will had. It was still the heaving, dirty cess-pit he'd always called it, but it was so familiar now that he felt it was a kind of home. He sniffed and, strangely, even welcomed the smell. In the Palace, he walked the panelled corridors to the kitchens, smelt the much more beautiful aroma of baking bread outside the bakery, and held his nose as he passed the Wet Room with all its fish. He might miss all this, but he had made his decision.

He opened the door of his former kitchen and saw again all the well-known faces he had left behind only months before. It was strange that the first thing he saw was that Derry had taken his place at the pottage table. It didn't matter. Tom looked immediately both pleased to see him and also distressed. He probably thinks I want my job back, thought Will.

'I'm just visiting,' he called out.

There were words of surprise and welcome. He was told he looked well. Everyone was impressed by how smart he looked in his good quality clothes. They were all pleased to see him. He did a tour of the room, sat in his old place by the turnspit and even turned the handle. Bessie hugged him and Gillie shook his hand vigorously. He stood quietly next to Kitty, aware that every eye in the room would be watching him. He thought they'd probably guessed how he felt about her.

'Perhaps I can see you later? I'll help you carry your rubbish to the midden.'

He spoke in almost a whisper but wondered if Derry would turn up later hiding in the bushes. He smiled. That didn't matter anymore.

He went into the great hall and had something to eat whilst he waited for the end of work time for the kitchen and then he made his way to the midden, not the most romantic of places but it would serve. He helped Kitty empty her bucket and then they sat down on that old tree trunk together.

'I'm glad to see you again,' she began and he told her about his journey, about his mother and about Lord Randolph. She had heard of the man but had never known of Will's connection with him. At least Derry hadn't splashed that piece of information all around. And then there was silence between them.

Will knew that this had to be the moment. He prayed that it would all work out how he hoped. He had no idea what he would do if it didn't. He took her hand and broke the silence.

'I have something to ask you, Kitty. Please listen and think carefully before you reply. I have a proposition to put to you. It will be an honest and honourable one. I'm hoping you'll accept. You will need to think long about it and ask me questions.'

THE VIEW FROM THE TURNSPIT

ACKNOWLEDGEMENTS

Thanks to my husband and daughter for their continual support and to my friends, Dianna and Chris Haggerty and Marie Mervill, who keep buying my books. I am grateful that you all show such faith in me.

On Mary Queen of Scots:

Antonia Fraser, Alison Weir, Jenny Wormald and John Guy.

I began a novel on Mary Queen of Scots years ago, which I later abandoned, but I researched and made notes then, which have perhaps helped me more than I realise. Thanks then are needed for G. Donaldson, Dr. Saul David, Iris Brooke, Madeleine Bingham, Marjorie Bowen, Stefan Zweig and H. Armstrong-Davisson.

Also by Sylvia Davey

Three novels about the persecution of the Cathars in Southern France, an heretical sect who lived in the Pyrenees in the thirteenth century. The novels are based on characters who really lived 700 hundred years ago. We know about their lives from their depositions at their inquisitional trials found in the Vatican Library. Google their names ... Pierre Clergue, Beatrice de Planissoles, Arnaud Sicre, Guillaume Belibaste.

Priest

Jumping From The Tower

Beatrice

All available from Amazon.

And if you would like to contact me:

Email: sylves@hotmail.co.uk

SYLVIA DAVEY

Printed in Great Britain
by Amazon